# Help, I'm going out with a jerk again!

I hope you will enjoy it! :)

Lots of Love! ♡

Riley Baker

# Riley Baker

**Help, I'm going out with a jerk again!**
**Copyright © 2019 by Riley Baker**

Published: Riley Baker 2019
rileybakerbooks@gmail.com
First published in Hungary by Colorcom Media 2014
Translator: Fanni Sütő
Editor: Anna Stekovics
Proofreading: Malik Crumpler
Photo by Laura Carlson of Lcphotoart
Model: Kendra Hatfield
Cover by Najla Qamber Designs

Six years is a very long time, especially when you're in a relationship.

Six years have gone by and I still think of you the same way. I'm before the most wonderful day of my life and I said yes. Yes to a life, that I've secretly wanted ever since I was a little girl.

Mum would always say that if the One walked in through the door, I shouldn't let him go, no matter how complicated life was, because we had only one life; only one to love and be loved. I'm very fond of my mum, her sayings and all her spontaneity. I believe in somebody turning up and changing everything. The prince from fairy tales, a carriage from fairy tales, life of fairy tales.

Six years is a long time even in a relationship only one of the parties knows about. In this case, I'm the concerned party.

The other party, well, I don't think he knows, just like I didn't know for a long time, until I remembered the beginning...

# Chapter One

He slowly traced his finger along my lips while he cupped my face in his hand. He ran his left hand through my hair and pulled me closer to him and planted a tiny kiss on the corner of my mouth. I would be lying if I denied that my entire body trembled from his touch.

My heart raced and I silently prayed that he wouldn't hear my heart's feverish beating. His lips idly traced the most sensitive areas of my neck. I tried to fight it, but my body couldn't put up a fight for long. And my mind... well, I lost my mind somewhere along the way, in-between two passionate kiss-fests as we tried to get into his flat. Finally, I gave in. *He is not like the others,* I told myself. *He really isn't!* I would be lying if I told you that my fairytale came true and we lived happily ever after. Maybe that would be the case, in romance novels, but not in real life.

His lips slowly moved towards mine, which was all fine and dandy, but with a sudden movement, god knows why, he thrust his tongue deep down my throat. I didn't know if I should try to get some air or somehow let him know that this tornado-effect was very off-putting.

But he really isn't like the others!

Every girl says this well-known sentence at least once, if not ten times, in her life. Then comes the slap in the face, the disappointment. It's like when you know there's something you shouldn't do, but you still do it, because you hope you're going to be the exception, the one that gets away with it. Of course, it never happens.

I reasoned with myself, listed points why I should or shouldn't do it. How ridiculous of me, to think that I had a say in any of this! He already had me, even before he noticed me across the bar. Of course, I wouldn't have admitted this to him.

I didn't care about his lame kissing stunt because his smile deleted "no" from my vocabulary. I have never been a fan of one-night stands. Actually, I was the dating-type. Dating gave me some kind of peace. You know how it is, you and your target go to the cinema at least twice and after, you go walking to the island, it makes you look less easy. Although, now that I think of it, there's not much difference, but I didn't care about all of that, back then. It's not like I'm going to meet him again. But that smile, oh, my god! Yes, it was that kind of smile that "makes your panties drop", smile. You know the kind where he doesn't need to say anything, promise anything, because in your head you've already thrown away your panties six times. I felt that he was dying to get me. I fell in love. At least in that moment.

He was 6'1 feet tall, his skin; a lighter shade of bronze and his eyes shone sea blue or forest green. He wasn't classically handsome, but he had a charm that could've landed him a role in any teen movie. He was the kind of guy who made women crazy and he wanted me, only me! I finally was spoken for. I was his, completely and without reservations. I could say I'd fallen in love, but it would be the same kind of hasty statement as my usual, "I swear he's not like the others" slogan. Maybe the illusion of being in love could save me from feeling guilty about being so easy. It wasn't the case, though. I was looking for love, but I felt like a complete idiot. I should've savoured the moment in which, he was there and he wanted only me, but somehow I couldn't. Of course, I couldn't because I knew our bond was just for one night.

I set my alarm clock to earlier than usual, so I'd have time to perform my "sneak out to the bathroom before he wakes up" girly ritual. *In those ten minutes I can make miracles!* Although it's completely pointless to play the ninja so early in the morning since I'll never see him again, but I just don't want him to tell his friends that he got completely wasted and the morning after almost fell out of bed from the shock of my unmade-up face. And not from my beauty.

A refreshing face wash, the tiniest bit of foundation, some toothpaste and voila! I snuggled back into bed with him, all innocent and pretended to be fast asleep. I got so carried away with my imagination that I ended up considering him my 52nd imaginary husband.

Unfortunately, the reality was this: the birdsong of my alarm clock filled the room with a horrible ruckus at that very moment. *If I've just dreamt this, then it's very possible that I have absolutely no make-up on and my hair looks like the fur of cats in heat. Help! Help! I need a Plan C!* Why has nobody written a manual about how to sneak out from the bed of a hot guy without being noticed? This could be the first entry: Gather your stuff quietly, without a sound, then make your way towards the door crawling, making sure to make the least noise possible. As a second step, we should try to open the door without it creaking. After this, we have two possible scenarios:

a, We succeeded

b, Or we didn't.

I think the majority of cases ends in scenario B, so the final advice of the book would be run!

Luckily, we were in my flat. Even better: my family was gone for the weekend. *For God's sake, I was a responsible, adult woman!* Or maybe just an adult or really, just responsible, or something along those lines. No make-up on, so what? Let's stay positive!

Judging from the amount of booze threw back yesterday, there was a considerable chance that most of it was still circulating in him. So, if last night he thought I was a "very attractive girl" to put it in his own words, then maybe today I could settle for being a "could be worse." He woke up, or at least he seemed to stir. I wiggled, hinting that I was also awake. My "He's not like the others" catchphrase lost its punch, when I noticed his boxers on the floor. Thousands of snapshots flashed through my mind of what my future life of laundry could be like if he was ever to be my husband. No, thank you very much. I tried not to kick him too hard, but I failed. Amidst his grumbling "let me sleep just a little bit more", he eventually woke up completely.

That's the moment when the awkward silence fell, the air froze and in one second, I became forty years older. After a seemingly endless waiting period, he managed to blurt out the magic words:

"Good morning!"

*That voice, oh heavens!* It was the nonchalant, but confident voice perfectly matching his bad boy style. Yes, it was the kind of voice that could ask you for a cup of coffee at any moment of the day and you'd run to fulfil his noble mission. To be honest, I don't know what kind of voice bad boys usually have, because in our circles, the height of badness was when someone didn't take out their rubbish. One thing was sure: if I had to choose a representative voice for bad guys, it would be his.

I tried to reply in my own nonchalant way:

"Same to you!"

Since I'd never had a random one-night stand before, I had no idea how I to behave. *Should I make him breakfast? I don't want anything from him. More importantly, I don't want to end up on his list with the title "It's not enough that I banged this loser, she also made me breakfast."* It was pointless to wrack my brain about my options because in a few seconds he spoke again, making my situation much easier.

"So, should I be saying something?"

Gosh, what a jerk! Is he really asking me if he should say something?

Suddenly his voice was much less sexy, shattering the image I had of him last night.

"Well, not necessarily, but I'd like to show you something. There's the way out!" With a careless movement of my hand I pointed to the door.

I managed to surprise myself with this not so very nice gesture. His jaw dropped to the floor. It didn't take long for me to realise that I was being a bit childish, since he didn't force me to spend the night with him and he didn't even use the typical lame pickup lines the others do: "We'll have three kids and a yacht on the Mediterranean and so on and so on." Actually he didn't promise me anything. I started to feel pretty embarrassed until I finally got over it, when the door slammed shut with the force customary in similar situations.

I didn't want to delve any deeper into my thoughts because I always wound up feeling like a complete idiot.

I checked my phone and I saw that I had forty-two missed calls. Forty-two! I'm not joking! I didn't even have to unlock it to know that it was my bestie, Ruby. Of course, I was right. It was half past twelve and I should have been in the park by the fountain like we'd agreed on, some days ago. I hadn't seen Ruby for two weeks, which seemed like an eternity because she'd always been an integral part of my life.

One time, when I was a kid, my family and I were driving back home from a family holiday, dad looked away from the road for a split second and we collided with another car.

In the opposite lane a black Ford tried to overtake someone, but it didn't work out.

Mum had a miscarriage. Back then I didn't really understand what happened. All I understood was that something bad had happened and my baby sister couldn't be born because of it. Nobody else was hurt in the accident, but it was enough to change a lot of things. Mum became a completely different person; something broke in her that day, in dad too. That's the day I first got to know Ruby. Dad didn't want me to go inside the hospital because he was worried that I might get anxious from all the things I'd see in there, so instead he had our new neighbours look after me. They took me in without a word and to my joy, I discovered their daughter who was the same age as me. From that day on, whenever I'd see dad with his heavy eyes hurry back to mum at the hospital, I began to see Ruby as some sort of angel, or like the sister I'd never have. To this day, this hasn't changed. I enjoyed spending time with Ruby even though she was my exact opposite. Yep, that's Ruby for you: the girl who drove men crazy and could care less about them. She didn't give a hoot about love, but the promise of a secure future with a rich guy, now that made her more eager than anything else in the world. I envied her because her heart hadn't been broken, unlike mine, which had been smashed to the ground, jumped on and crushed at least sixty times already. As a matter of fact, the only time I remember Ruby expressing some sign of emotions over anything, was when her bank card was put on hold. Despite all of that, you just had to love her, even though she was convinced that Voldemort was played by Kevin Costner.

Ruby had a "secret" half-brother, who came to visit them every three years or so. We rarely talked about him, for me, it was as if he didn't even exist, especially since I'd never met him. Sadly, whenever he would come to visit Ruby's family, I was always away at summer camp or on a family holiday, so I never met the mysterious boy.

Ruby was full of enthusiasm and told me that her half brother would be staying with her family until the end of the summer holiday so she wanted us to finally meet. I agreed, without hesitation. Ruby got so immersed in her story about her adventure with the surfer guy from last night, that I managed to completely forget about mine. Of course, mine was nowhere near as interesting as hers. I even considered remaining silent about my uninteresting little fling last night, but Ruby would have none of that:

"So what's up with you? Come on, out with the details! I want to hear your big story too!"

"Big story? It's really not that interesting."

"The others told me you were out in Hell's last night."

Great, I was too naïve to think I could get away with it.

"To be honest, nothing interesting happened."

"Come on, Amy, don't be like that! First of all, I know you to well. Second, our other friends messaged me that you left with some tall, handsome guy around midnight. So, what should I know about him?"

Thank you, guys! I can consider myself lucky that they didn't post it on social media too.

"Yeah, he was tall alright, and the rest... Well, his name is: Jerk. Age: Unknown to me, just like any other personal information about him. What is done cannot be undone, but let's not waste another word on him because he was just awful, like the whole night."

Luckily Ruby didn't pry for more details, because her phone rang.

"We're a bit late with the newspaper. When can you come over and start working on it? I'll finally introduce you to my half-brother."

Ruby and I ran the local newspaper, well we were in charge of around eighty percent of it. Okay, okay, to be completely honest, we just had a tiny part in it, a monthly column. Ruby babbled about fashion while I scribbled about love in hopes to brighten the day of our little community with my embarrassing stories. Ruby's dad was in charge of the editorial board, so we were always allowed to publish articles, about anything that hopefully interested young people. For some strange reason (unbeknownst to us) whatever we came up with, the locals loved it. So writing for the local newspaper was perfect work experience for me, beside college. We were slowly walking to Ruby's place while trying to come up with new columns for the newspaper like "Where can you party on after the bar is closed?" "Design your dream outfit: cheap and chic!" We had a lot of great ideas by the time we arrived. We were pottering around in the kitchen, when I heard a familiar voice behind our back:

"Hey, girls!"

*Oh no, I was sure I'd already heard this voice somewhere before.* The feeling of recognition hit me like a landslide and sweat rolled down my forehead. Oh boy, I was in trouble. I didn't dare turn around because the voice was too much like the one from yesterday: *"So should I be saying something?"*

# Chapter Two

Despite all of my efforts to avoid the voice, I had to respond, even though I was frozen to the spot in which I stood, embarrassed or maybe even ashamed. In that moment, I discovered new depths to the meaning of this phrase because before I had trouble imagine how someone could be frozen to the spot. Well, now I got it, like this! Ruby tapped my shoulder.

"Amy, let me introduce you to Adam."

Please, let it not be him, please, please, please!

Ah, so Adam it is. Good to know the Jerk has a name.

I looked at Ruby, then Adam, then back to Ruby and, as calmly as possible I tried to send emergency signals to my brain that I should immediately stop shaking my head. Hoping to break the awkward silence, Ruby said:

"Hey, Adam, Amy was just telling me that she'd had a run in with a completely infantile jerk yesterday."

The only thing worse than awkward silence is an awkward conversation. I wished the ground would open up under my feet and swallow me and my shame, whole. *Ruby, just shut up, please!*

I tried to send her telepathic signals, hoping that she'd understand from my furtive glances that it was high time she shut her pie-hole, but my sneaky attempts completely failed. Oh well, what were the chances he understand she was talking about him? I could've met other guys that night, before I met him. Noticing my reddening face, Ruby tried to ease the mood "further."

"Don't worry, Amy. Adam was telling me a similar story

before I went over to your place. He also managed to hook up with an idiot, last night."

Idiot, me? Oh well, Mr. Should-I-Say-Something.

I stepped closer, with what I hoped was nonchalance and held out my polite greeting hand.

"Please, forgive me, dear Adam, you probably missed my name yesterday: Amy, a.k.a. the idiot."

The retort was imminent.

"My deepest excuses, my lady, I was also most impolite during the course of last night. My name is Adam, you know the Jerk from last night."

I think the only person who felt more awkward than us was Ruby.

"Did you two sleep together?"

I was preparing my answer, but Adam was quicker.

"No."

A smug half-smiled appeared on his lips. I had trouble interpreting his smile because it could have meant, "Thank god, no" or "not, yet." Although our mutual dislike for one another, made me think the first option was the most likely. Ruby left us alone for a little while, saying that she'd take our notes upstairs while we talked it out. I knew very well that meant she'd leave me some time to gather the remains of my pride and shame, from the floor. Anything, but that! I didn't dare to look him in his eyes, now that it was clear that we had two completely different versions of the same night. What could he possibly think about me? I'm just some stupid girl who got so drunk last night that she wound up having delusions, or, even worse, he thinks I wanted to show off to my friends by telling people I'd slept with him.

I had to stop my wild derailed, train of thought because suddenly he was standing beside me. There was no way I'd be able to avoid his gaze.

*Calm down, Amy, be cool!* He doesn't know what to tell women the morning after, and you don't know what to tell guys after nothing happened.

I had no idea what was coming next. Maybe he'd laugh in my face and call me a naïve little thing for believing something had happened between us or maybe he'd just tell me to go to hell for making up things about him, to Ruby.

He leaned so close to me that I almost felt his breath on my face. If it hadn't been him, the moment could've been romantic. When I was getting quite used to the situation, he lifted his left arm and reached above my shoulder to get a glass from the cupboard.

Of course! He poured himself a glass of water then grabbed a huge book entitled "Unicorns on the battle field" from the counter and headed for the door. He looked back at me one last time before he walked out. I waited a bit for the air to clear, then I went up the stairs.

Unicorns on the battle field. Goodness gracious! I'm so surprised he doesn't know what to tell women the morning after?

After the Jerk left, I was afraid to go up and talk with Ruby, even though I'd prepared myself for her possible rejection and judgement. To my surprise, she welcomed me with:

"Amy, I hope you don't have a crush on him."

"Ruby, I'd like to assure you that I don't care about him at all, so chill! Even if he was the last man on Earth, I wouldn't care less. I just hooked up with him in because I was drunk, in any other circumstances I would've just walked past him. "

Of course, Amy, you need to convince yourself first, before you can convince others!

"Amy, please. I've known you since forever. Whenever you call a guy an idiot, it means we're going to spend the next few days plotting about ensnaring him in order to forget him. You could have any guy in the world, but you have this weird attraction to the kind of bad boys that any normal girl does all she can to avoid. "

"Ruby, calm down! That period of my life is over and I'd like to reassure you again, that I don't give the slightest damn about Adam."

But Ruby was Ruby, nothing could stop her, she just went on and on. In a mere half an hour I managed to gather from her, Adam's life story, that he wasn't into relationships and

14

he'd never been in love, just like most of the hunting men like himself. What an unexpected twist!

I tried to stop Ruby from telling me anything else about Adam, because I really didn't care about him. I wasn't in love with him, on the contrary, I was in love with being in love. Thanks to this fact, I managed to get over most of my disappointments in a matter of a few days. I knew that the only way to calm Ruby down, was to give in and go on a date with this other guy, Aaron. He was in his last year of school, one year above us. He was captain of the football team and our local heartthrob. Girls were all over Aaron, (quite literally) and female hearts rained down on him wherever he went. He was also as tall as a ladder, almost 6'5 and his muscular body was ripped. As a tiny piece of extra information, I'd also like to add that he was my first real kiss back in summer camp during middle school. Honestly, it was more like a peck on the lips, but still. Ruby was convinced that Aaron had been in love with me ever since. Every day at lunch break his fan club lined up at the table to faithfully wait for Aaron to walk past them all red and sweaty, after his training. It was similar to women who swoon in front of the TV screen when a guy emerges from a swimming pool in slow motion.

Every year for my birthday, to show off how romantic he is, he asks me out. To which I, true to myself, always reply with "Sorry, but I'm busy." He's handsome, yeah really hot, as if he just climbed out of this year's Calvin Klein ad'… But yeah, there's always that stupid but. *That's it, there're no more buts, Amy!* We're going on a date, with Aaron.

Of course during the following days I never managed to cross his path, although I did everything I could to run into him. For example, I didn't hide in the girl's restroom to prevent him from finding me. Ruby's great idea was that I should ask Aaron for help with one of my articles. What's more, he could even be the subject of my article with his heartthrob lifestyle. Then, like in fairy tales, we'd fall into each other's arms and the curse that had been upon me for so long, would finally break and the successions of idiots would be finally over.

Friday night, we planned to go the cinema with Ruby and Violet, who was also an important person in my life. Not as much as Ruby, but she was right below her on my list of important people. Violet was an energy bomb, she lived for parties. Party, after party after party. So you can imagine my surprise, when she announced that LOVE (the big one, in all capital letters) had found her. Knowing her, we were convinced that this new love would only last for about two weeks, like all the other candidates had. She cried to us about how her newest victim would fly back to Greece in two weeks, leaving our freshly enamoured Violet behind.

*A magical two weeks.*

A real pity indeed, but I didn't want to disappoint Violet by telling her that if she stayed with him much longer, then it would be her who put the poor guy on the first plane back home. I love Violet, but I just can't imagine her in a serious relationship.

We waited and waited at Ruby's place because our Violet was late again. We hadn't decided what to watch yet, but we usually went for some seemingly lame horror movie that inevitably kept us awake all night. We loved horror movies and the feeling that after it, we didn't even dare go downstairs, least we come across a ghost, a curse, or anything we'd seen in the film that night.

In the meantime, Violet sent us a "Sorry, I'm going to be late." text and I sneaked out to the kitchen to make us all some ice cream. I heard some noise outside and since I knew Ruby's parents weren't home, I knew it could only be one person. I wanted to turn back as quietly as possible, but when I put my foot down to step through the threshold the floor let out an enormous creak.

"Hey, Amy!"

He noticed you. It's best to say hello.

"Oh, he-hey, Adam!"

He had that obnoxious smile again, the one he'd wear even

if a teacher told him he failed every subject and needed to redo his entire third year. He'd still stand there, with the same proud, stupid face, looking at the teacher and jovially proclaiming that alright, he'd retake the whole year.

In his hand, I noticed a cereal bowl decorated with a dragon. He looked quite lame. Okay, that's a lie. He was shirtless. He must've just come back from running because he was a bit sweaty and if I wanted to be honest, and why wouldn't I, he looked pretty hot.

I tried not to pay him any attention and instead walked deliberately towards the fridge until I noticed what kind of cereal he was eating. It was my favourite! I hadn't eaten it since I was a small child. Where can you even buy it these days and why is he eating it? He can't be eating my favourite cereal! It was made of oats with sugar around the edges and it was so good you could even eat it without milk. Well, at least I could. I really thought it wasn't produced anymore, but apparently it was because he had his. But how? Lost in my thoughts, I must have been staring at him blankly for too long.

"Are you okay, Amy? You can have some if you want."

Jesus, I must have been pretty obvious if he had to comment about my staring.

"Oh, no, thanks. And yeah. I mean I'm fine."

"Are you sure? Because Barty, my puppy gives me that look when he's hungry."

"It's very nice of you to compare me to your dog, but I'm not begging you for food, I've just got lost in my thoughts."

"You should try it though, it's the coolest cornflakes ever! It was my favourite as a child, but then it was discontinued. At least I thought it was, but then I saw it in one of the shops at the airport and I bought like four boxes. Are you sure you don't want to taste it?"

*Are you sure you don't want to shut up? "You should really try it!" Oh, how nice and caring somebody has suddenly become.* Was it really his favourite too? That's impossible, unimaginable, I refuse to accept that possibility. I, and my future husband, can be the only ones that love that cereal. In my imagination, that's exactly the part when me and my Mr. Big realise that we both love the same cereal and that means even the heavens have decided we're destined for each other. Adam ruined this image for me.

"Surely not."

I refuse to eat from his food after he basically called me a dog-face. Anyway, it's no longer my favourite cereal, now that I know it's his favourite too. My mouth won't water anymore when I think of having a little bite of my favourite cereal, no not at all, anymore. I took the ice cream from the fridge, that was my original mission after all, then I left the kitchen completely ignoring him.

Violet was almost a half an hour late, so we considered leaving without her because almost all the good films already started or were just about to start at the cinema. At the last minute, Violet arrived. She brought the rain clouds with her. For weeks, the radio had been predicting big storms. I hurried upstairs for my coat and ran into Adam on the way down. When I say "ran into Adam," I mean it literally. I bumped into him, but he just smiled and didn't say anything. He must've considered me to be the lamest girl in the universe. I murmured a sorry, when he suddenly grabbed my arm.

"Barty has the cutest eyes in the world, just for your information."

What the hell is that supposed to mean? His dog is cute, good for him!

On the way to the cinema all I could think about was why he gave me that cheesy dog talk. Who the hell cares about his dog or him? I couldn't share my thoughts with Ruby because the official stand point was that I didn't care about him at all. I really didn't.

By the time we got to the cinema, the only movies we hadn't missed were an action movie and a half lame horror flick. It wasn't even a question of which one we would choose: the latter. Violet was as good as absent, we lost her at the beginning of the film and she kept texting her Greek Adonis the whole movie. Two boys sat right next to us. One of them had long brown hair and who knows what colour his eyes were, I couldn't see in the dark, but he wasn't really my style, so I didn't try to take a better look. The other one had dark brown hair, shaved on the sides. Ruby had been exchanging flirty looks with one of them since the movie started. For once, I was only interested in the film and figuring out why Adam told me about his dog. Stop! I can't care about anything related to him.

The film was the exact quality we'd expected. You could watch it once, if you were really bored and had nothing better to do. Even though it's main character was a pretty scary creature. After watching horror movies we usually had a sleepover at Ruby's and left all the lamps on while we slept, to keep the monsters away. On the way out of the cinema, one of the two guys asked Ruby for her number and suggested we go on a double date with them, because his friend liked me.

Ruby said yes without waiting for my answer. I didn't mind that much because that way I didn't need to hunt down Aaron or suffer through the date alone. Violet didn't give a hoot about being left out from the whole double-date thing.

I hated dating. I hated the feeling that you didn't know the other person, you didn't know how to behave or what to say. Okay, be yourself, but then? If you give yourself a hundred times and still nobody wants you, you start to think that there's something wrong with you. Then comes the self-help thoughts, like one day your Prince Charming will come and you'll be perfect for him. Sure, sure, but where is he? His horse must have broken down.

Ruby had set up a date for the next day, even before we got home. On the way home Violet grilled Ruby about Adam.

"Ruby, where have you been hiding Adam? Amy, have you noticed how hot he is?" She laughed then continued.

"If I'd known that you were fixing me up with such a hottie, I'd have packed up my boyfriend on the first plane today."

Of course Violet was joking, but we know very well that there is a grain of truth in every joke.

"I don't think, he is that handsome, though," I said before Violet melted in the back seat from her tirade. Ruby looked at me and smiled, but said nothing. Nothing at all and that was pretty suspicious. Maybe I've managed to convince her that I really didn't care. Or maybe I've proved just the opposite. *What am I saying? I really don't care.* Trying to change subject, I stirred the conversation towards our upcoming date.

"Those two guys were pretty cute, right?"

Ruby sat in silence, giving me a measly, "yes." I felt like she was angry with me even though I did absolutely nothing wrong. At least I don't think I did. Has she got upset because I said that Adam was no big deal? She knows he is. Everybody who has eyes, knows.

Violet faked a stomach ache and asked us to take her home although we both knew she just wanted to spend the night with her newest conquest.

We were on our way home when the storm got worse. It only took five seconds for us to run inside the house, but it wasn't enough to prevent us from getting soaked. We laughed. We stood there drenched, smelling of rain, just like when we were kids and didn't care about the water ruining our hair. As adults, we had a different stance on rain, it became our biggest enemy because a few drops were enough to make us look like stray dogs.

Adam was still awake, watching some series in the living room when we arrived. We must have been a sight to behold and of course he couldn't help but remark:

"Was the film so romantic that you started to melt? Ha-ha."

What a great joke, Adam, thank you very much! Do you really want a statue for the Grand Master of Humour?

Ruby ignored his comment.

"I don't really remember the film because we had two cute guys sitting next to us," she replied to Adam's teasing.

"Did it make the film less shit?" Adam asked arching his eyebrow.

"Yep, because we're going on a date with them."

"We?"

"Yes, we're going on a double date with Amy."

His smile melted away, I could hardly believe my eyes. He

tried to feign nonchalance, saying "cool," then he bid us goodnight and left for bed. We changed into our pyjamas with Ruby and tried to select our outfits for our wonderful double date. I didn't care at all about the whole thing, I only agreed to it because I wanted to convince Ruby that I didn't want anything from Adam. It was true, even though I thought about him a lot.

I kept tossing and turning the whole night because I knew I should be concentrating on tomorrow's date, giving a new chance to another loser to break my heart or prove that it's not my fault and I'm not damned for the rest of my entire life.

I have to drink something or I'll dry out.

My stomach hurt which wasn't a good sign because it always meant that something unpredictable would happen and I didn't want anything unpredictable happening in my life. Except for the arrival of my Prince Charming, of course.

"Ruby, I'm going downstairs to drink something because I'm not feeling well."

She didn't answer me because she'd been sleeping for hours, I guess. Her love life wasn't a disaster like mine, she had nothing to toss and turn about in bed. I was afraid to go downstairs in the dark because the creature from the film that attacked its victims in the dark would find this occasion ideal for ambushing me. I plucked up my courage and made my way downstairs. I didn't turn the lights on because I didn't want to wake Ruby or Adam. The stairs squeaked as I gently stepped on them. My heart thumped loudly because I was afraid that something would attack me in the dark. Well done, Amy, why are you watching stupid movies if they keep you up at night? In the cinema I felt like a big girl, but not anymore. I tried to ignore the voices in my head. In the end, I got downstairs safe and sound and poured a glass of water. I felt a presence behind my back and refused to turn around completely. I dropped my glass and let out such a loud shriek that I think even the neighbours heard me, luckily they didn't call the police on me.

"Chill, Amy, it's just me, Adam!"

He put his hand over my mouth as he pulled me to himself

to calm me. I hit him so hard, a street fighter would've envied my punch.

"Are you out of your mind? What are you doing here? You know that…"

My voice was so shaky I could barely finish telling him that he scared me shitless.

"I know and I'm sorry. I didn't mean to scare you. Please forgive me, my lady, but I've become thirsty and I was so impertinent to come down and drink. I promise it won't happen again."

I felt that I was a bit rude to him, he'd just got thirsty in the middle of night, of course at the exact same time as I did but that was beside the point.

"Sorry for punching you. But if I told you I didn't mean it, I'd be lying. You really scared me."

"Am I that ugly?"

"You're not ugly at all. Actually, yes you are. I mean, no. It wasn't your looks that scared me, but the film we watched with the girls tonight."

"Don't worry, I was just pulling your leg."

I poured him some water after I cleaned up the shards of glass I'd broken.

"Are you looking forward to tomorrow's double date?"

What is the perfect answer for this? Honesty. Honesty is always the best policy, so I answered accordingly.

"Sure! They're quite cute."

Alright, so we can't always follow the best policy because it's not always easy to be as honest as we'd want to, but I didn't dare tell him that neither the guy, nor the date interested me at all. Actually, at that particular moment I couldn't care about anything else other than thinking about him, and that really scared me.

"Cool. So, what's his name?"

"His?"

"I guessed your date was a guy. Does he have a name?"

Oops. What's his name actually? I can't make up a fake name because tomorrow Ruby would bust me, in a second."

"Sure he has a name, but why do you care?"

Best defence is offence. Now, let us nicely bid him goodnight so he won't discover that I have no idea whatsoever, about the name of that unfortunate soul.

"Nothing, I was just curious."

"Great. I'm exhausted though, so I'll go back to sleep, okay?"

"Sure thing, sweet dreams. But if I can give you one piece of good advice, before the date ask Ruby what his name is. I'm sure he'd feel hurt if you said something like "Hey, you!""

*Busted!* But how? How could he know? Are all of my thoughts clearly visible on my face or did Ruby forget to tell me that this guy's a mind reader? That would be pretty embarrassing for me, because then he'd know that my feelings for him have been pretty hectic for the last twenty-four hours. "Sweet dreams!" How could I have sweet dreams when you're being so much sweeter? And you shouldn't be! At least not for me.

There was no point in denying that there was something in him. Something that attracted and repulsed me away at the same time. Maybe it's always been like this, when you hate someone because you could love them. I looked for pros and cons. There were two hundred and eighty against him and for him there was just one, but that one triumphed over all the other two hundred and eighty counter arguments. That one argument for him, was the fact that I had a crush on him. A huge, ugly, crush.

# Chapter Three

It was just a stupid little flame. There was no fire here, none at all. Fire burns and trap you, while tiny flames flicker out of existence as if they'd never existed to begin with. Me and him? No way. No freaking chance. Impossible. So, I buried Adam and my feelings about him, deep within myself.

Summer holidays ended a full week ago and Adam was still living at Ruby's. I didn't dare ask him any questions about any of it, least I'd reveal my dirty little secret.

What dirty little secret? It's just a flame, Amy, a tiny, insignificant flame!

I spent the first week of school hiding from Aaron. Ruby of course had no idea about it. Poor naïve thing, she was of the firm belief that I was trying to hunt down Aaron for an interview which served no other goal than bringing us closer to each other. However, now that she found me another victim, I didn't have to worry about Aaron anymore so I could finally relax a bit.

The next evening, Ruby called me around six because the boys were supposed to pick us up in two hours. I fished out a short, torn pair of jeans from the bottom of my wardrobe and complemented it with a simple white top and white sneakers. I didn't want to look overdressed, quite the contrary. This was the perfect "be myself" outfit. I didn't care about anybody's opinion of me, not even Ruby's who commented on my ensemble:

"That's what you're wearing on the date?"

I knew it wasn't a question, but a hidden message that I had only ten minutes left if I wanted to change. But I didn't.

"Yep, this is my dating outfit."

"Alright. I think someone is going to spend the night at home alone."

*I think someone is secretly praying for the very same thing as she is.* To be honest, I didn't want anything else other than staying at home in my favourite purple leggings and watching the latest episode of Vampire Diaries while jealously thinking about Elena, who managed to tame the bad boy who loves her, like nobody could ever love me. That's what I really wanted to do all night with some hazelnut chocolate. Was that really too much to ask for?

I asked Ruby and the guys to meet at my place because I knew once Adam saw my face he'd see through me, right away. I don't know why but I had the feeling that he really knew me, of course he actually didn't.

Ruby was completely dolled up as if she'd prepared for her wedding. The boys arrived in time. Ruby's date wanted to go bowling. I didn't consider this a real date- so I can't call the guy for me, *my date*. Let's just say, the other guy that I was paired with, wanted to go to the cinema. He also had a name: Christian. Ruby looked at me with begging eyes, and I got what she meant: I was supposed to go to the cinema with Christian while she went bowling with the other guy. There goes the double date. I had no idea what Ruby liked about this guy, he was such a slime ball. Okay, yes he was handsome, but that didn't matter because he was so full of himself that his huge ego knocked everybody out. He was the kind of guy who, if you were mugged when you were together, he'd throw you at the attacker just to save himself. Manliness: zero.

I won't say anything about my plus one. Of course, my hostility might be largely due to the fact that the only person I could have had any possible fun with was Adam. I said goodbye to Ruby and her guy then got in the car next to Christian. Cinema seemed like a good choice for us because at least I wouldn't have to talk to him during the movie. The whole ride to the Cinema, all he talked about was his football career and how lucky I was to go out with him tonight because at his school, girls fight over him. Of course they do,

I can only imagine!

I already saw the headlines of my newest article: *What happens when his ego is bigger than his IQ?* The subject of our article is about an infamous womaniser and seducer: Christian. The big question came up as soon as we arrived at the cinema: what should we see? I voted for a girly movie, because I didn't want to suffer tonight like I did last night, after yesterday's horror movie. He wanted us to see some stupid action film. In the end he made it clear that since he paid, he'd choose. *What a knight in shining armour!* If it hadn't happened to me, I wouldn't believe it. Sadly, I know myself enough to admit that I always attracted the biggest jerks. I should be proud of myself, a newer success. A new jerk, a new chapter. Our gentleman wasn't joking, he bought the two tickets for the blockbuster entitled Dingo, the hero. Inside myself, I was dying laughing at the fact that if I'd chosen the film, we'd be in two different screenings and later we'd discuss the separate movies we'd seen. What was he thinking, honestly? Yesterday's impression of him rapidly moved towards disgust. I cursed Ruby because it was all her fault. I cursed her because she got me into this whole mess, but I also cursed myself because I let her. In the end, I didn't contest his decision and followed Christian into the auditorium for the immature action film. He was the only one in the whole cinema who laughed at the pitiful jokes, I couldn't wait for the film to be over so I could give Ruby a piece of my mind for ruining my evening. Sadly, the film was way too long. I rethought my whole life three times while I watched it, focusing on every minute I could remember, trying to let go of all the thoughts about wishing Christian would drown in his giant popcorn box – he'd only bought one for himself, because as he said, girls shouldn't eat this kind of shit. *How attentive!* The biggest piece of shit in the whole cinema was Christian himself, but at least now I could pass on the title of the biggest jerk from Adam to Christian. He really deserved it. As soon as the film was over, I used Violet's fake stomach ache excuse and demanded Christian take me home. Surprisingly enough, he seemed quite sad and begged me to sit with him somewhere so he could get to know me better. In the beginning, I thought it was my fault and he was rude to me because he didn't like me either, but I finally understood that it wasn't the case. He was just born rude. Unfortunately for him, I had no wish to get to know him better, so I faked the stomach ache even more convincingly just to get rid of him. He didn't protest anymore and took me home (to Ruby's place because I wanted to tell her off).

I told Christian that I couldn't find my house keys so I couldn't get into my flat so I'd have to spend the night at my friend's. He misunderstood me, being the gentleman that he was, and right away, offered that I could sleep at his place. I "the lucky chosen one" happily passed on his offer. It's flattering and everything, but no thanks.

At eleven o'clock, I was banging on Ruby's door, demanding to be let in. However, it wasn't her who opened the door. The one I managed to forget about during the evening's misery was now standing before me, in the doorway. Yes, Adam. I didn't know it could get any worse, but it had. I managed to make it obvious for him that my date with Christian was horrid and that's why I was back so early. But whenever you ask yourself the question of how could it possibly get any worse, something much, much worse inevitably comes your way. I didn't even have to wait long for it. I heard steps behind me and when I turned around I saw Christian. He figured that we'd continue getting to know each other over lunch the next day. I was embarrassed as hell because Adam knew how I really felt about this moron. I knew that he knew because a smile spread over his lips. Luckily Adam kept it under control otherwise he might have laughed in Christian's face. I think my expression must have clearly shown that I didn't want any kind of lunch and if I had any say in the matter, there would never be another date. I started mumbling like an idiot when Adam called out from behind my back.

"Amy, baby, it's good that you're back. But who's this guy with you?"

Christian seemed completely uncomfortable, he had no

idea what was going on. Me neither, but I didn't care.

Has he just called me baby?

Breaking the awkward silence Adam spoke again:

"Have I interrupted something? Sorry, man, but she's taken. I guess Miss Amy forgot to tell you about this."

Then he shifted his eyes at me and started shouting:

"Amy, get into the house right now!"

Christian asked in a trembling voice:

"Did you make me bring you home to your boyfriend?"

His face became so red that he could have switched careers from football to being a poster model, drawing attention to the overuse of sunbeds. In less than two minutes he was gone, the tires of his Mercedes screeched as he fled. I didn't even care about what Adam said to Christian because he literally saved me from him. He literally read my mind, again and although I didn't know how he did it or why he decided to help me, it didn't matter.

Did he really say "baby"? Am I his baby?

However grateful I felt, I still tried to hide it because we were speaking of Adam. Trying to protect my honour, I murmured my thanks and a silly sentence like, " I didn't need your help to get rid of him," then I went inside. He let out a sceptical laugh, "Sure thing" and followed me in.

"Is Ruby home?" I asked.

Why would she be home? I'm sure her date wasn't as catastrophic as mine.

"No, she isn't. What do you say, dear "not so dear" Amy, if we discussed it tomorrow at lunch while we got to know each other a bit better."

"You're very funny, Adam!"

"I'm not being funny. What do you say to actually having a hamburger right now? You could tell me about your dream date with your nightmare guy. Ruby won't be home for another two hours or so, anyway.

*Adam and me, eating out together?* My legs will tremble so much that I'll collapse on the way.

"You know there's a hamburger place at the foot of the bridge that's open late. We'll walk there and back and Ruby may even be home, by the time we get back. Only if you feel like it, of course. "

If I feel like it? Can't you see my heart jumping out of its place?

"Yeah, I know where it is. Let's go, I'm starving. Wouldn't you be disturbed by the fact that I'm eating junk food?"

"No, because you're doing it with me."

*Oh my gosh, isn't that almost flirting?* Now, I could be the one modelling on those sunbed posters with my red face.

I always loved walks on the shore at night. I was in love with the soft lights and soft rumbling waves of the lake. It was all very different walking here with someone like Adam. I know the cautionary tales Ruby told me about him, but I wasn't afraid. I knew should've been terrified of my feelings because I shouldn't have felt like this for him this early, but still. Has it ever happened to you that you didn't want anything else, but to be with that particular other person? It doesn't matter if he was a good or bad person, if you knew him or not. All that mattered was that you loved him and you could do nothing to stop it and to be honest, you didn't even want to. That's how I felt when I was with him. I didn't know anything about him, except for the things Ruby said about him. Contrary to everything she said, he showed me a completely different side of his personality. This is the side I fell in love with. Maybe he had darkness in him, but I didn't care because the part of him he showed me made the rest nicer.

It took a short time to realise that all I knew about Adam was from Ruby. We walked for maybe an hour, but it seemed like years to me. Among other things, Adam told me that no girls had ever managed to really interest him, so he didn't take them seriously and, however improbable it sounded, his heart had also been broken. He would give anything for a girl who could make him laugh, and that he could really talk to about anything, a girl who was spontaneous and who wouldn't plan every moment of her life in advance, a girl that lives in the moment, a girl who'd make his life better. *Hey, this could be me, couldn't it?*

We talked about the losers I've met and my goals in life. However strange it may sound, it was the first time I ever spoke this openly about my life anyone, let alone with him. I knew that I could say anything to him and he'd understand and he wouldn't judge me. Usually on dates I could never be myself, I was just a girl who wanted love and wanted it fast. That wasn't the case now. Maybe because it wasn't actually a date or was it that he really wasn't like all the others?

It took us one and a half hours to cover the half an hour long walk to the burger place. Luckily, there wasn't a very long queue. As usual, I asked for my burger without condiments, only with meat which earned me a loud laugh from Adam. We walked slowly backwards. I tried to eat in an elegant, not hamster-like manner, when suddenly Adam turned to me and gave me a curious look.

"So what happened on your date, don't think you can get away without telling me about it!"

"I was just starting to like you, but I guess that's the end of that."

"Well, then consider it revoked. Tell me about your first week at school then."

His eyes gleamed and a typical "half smile a la Adam" played on his lips.

I couldn't really tell him that my first week ended up being pretty hectic, for some strange reason unknown to even myself, I fell for him and to throw Ruby off, I had to date Aaron. However, I spent my first week avoiding him like a ninja, although Ruby had no idea about it. Also, I've been wondering for days why he was still at Ruby's? The deal was, that by the end of the summer break he'd be gone and I'd continue my lame dating life without him distracting me. Thinking all this over, I found it easier to answer the original question.

"Nothing extra, he's not my type."

"Well, well. He was yesterday, wasn't he?"

I knew he wouldn't leave it alone without commentary.

"Okay, Adam, you've won. Yesterday was yesterday and today is today. That boy was a disaster."

"So much so, that you had to literally run away from him? Isn't it possible that you're as picky with guys as you are with your food?"

*Picky?Me?* I'm not picky at all. I can't help it that I always end up with the rejects. I'm starting to feel uncomfortable, being an open book for you. From now on, I'll keep my secrets under lock and key.

"I don't know why I should discuss it with you of all people, but if you really want to know that guy was a jackass."

"Right, so he's a jackass and I'm a jerk, is that it?"

I felt as if he stood up for the whole male-kind, which I couldn't really understand because Christian was really, truly a jackass. *Okay, I was wrong about Adam, he's not a jerk, but the exception proves the rule, right?*

"No, Adam, you aren't a jerk. You're actually pretty decent compared to Christian, for example."

"Thanks for the compliment, but that's not what I meant, maybe if you were a bit nicer to boys, they'd be nicer to you. You ever thought about it that way?"

In the meantime, we arrived at Ruby's house. I think I have never ever been rude to Adam. *Okay, maybe in the beginning, and that last time, but I was pretty nice to him today, so I didn't understand his complaint.* The lights weren't on in the house, which meant Ruby was not yet home.

"Yeah, you must be right. It's my fault that nobody wants me."

"That's not what I said, Amy, no need to get offended."

"I didn't get offended, but if you didn't just sit at home all day reading your unicorn nonsense then maybe you'd learn how to communicate with girls, normally."

"Unicorn nonsense? That's the last manuscript my granddad left behind and it means a lot to me. I'm sorry if it seems stupid to you. But from now on I'll only read those *10 tips to guys* columns you write even though, you can't keep a guy because you chase all of them away, even the ones obviously head over heels for you. They just never make moves on you because of your attitude. Good night!"

He slammed the door shut. Again. *Déjà vu.*

I'm such an idiot! He was right in everything he said. I always attack, protecting myself. What right did I have to judge him? I wanted to apologise, but I was so embarrassed it felt like the best idea was running away. I couldn't sleep all night. I tossed and turned in bed until five in the morning, sometimes kicking off my blanket, sometimes pulling it over my head. He was completely right, I wrote my stupid articles giving advice about love without actually knowing anything about it.

Of course I wanted love in my life more than anything else, this wasn't my problem. The problem was that I was waiting for Prince Charming with his super-abilities but unfortunately for me, Amor's arrow always delivered me mere humans. The bane of romantic comedies and novels. We want perfection, but if it doesn't arrive to our life as we imagined it, then it shouldn't come at all. We always ignore the one who's been fighting for us for years but the one who is obviously a bad choice for us, always finds us with open arms.

Let's take Aaron for example. He's been chasing after me for years and I shun him each and every time. Then there's his perfect counterexample: Dylan. I could honestly say that he was the first big love in my life- I should really put it like this: he was my first misstep, the king of jerks and then after him, an army of jerks followed in a series of unfortunate events.

Dylan and I went out during the first year of high school, for a whole month. In the beginning everything was perfect. I secretly thanked the heavens that they made me such a lucky girl, I'd found the man of my dreams at such a tender age while most people never find him. I believed he'd be my husband, the father of my children, the man who could change me for the better and inspire me to learn to cook. I was wrong. The others told me in the beginning that he brandished all the "You should avoid me in your own best interest" signs, but I didn't believe them. "I'm going to change him!" I thought. Sure thing. I didn't suspect anything, even on our first date when we went to the cinema and he suggested that we go Dutch. What a cheap guy. But that was Dylan! We all know love is blind. I felt so special, but I wasn't, at least not because of Dylan. Strangely enough, I was the only one who didn't get suspicious that I only met him once per week outside of school. A little help for jerk-magnets like myself: he had two other girlfriends. I swear I tried everything! I tried to be secretive, so that I would become intriguing and he would spend the rest of his life trying to figure me out. I tried to be funny like in films where the perfect girlfriend always makes her target male laugh. Every now and again I had to shine in the role of the badass girl because I needed something else besides being funny. I also trained my understanding side, so when he was complaining about how wasted he'd got the previous night and he had to clean the whole flat even though he was so exhausted, I, the understanding girlfriend ran to him and cleaned up for him. How stupid I was! Dylan never considered me to be a woman, in his eyes I was just a silly high school girl with two cherry stones instead of boobs. It didn't take me long before I left him for good. Okay, actually he dumped me and I cried over him for months. I firmly believed he'd come back to me because we belonged together. He never came back and I'm not waiting for him anymore.

Getting back to my current heart throb, Adam knew how to communicate with girls. He managed to really talk to me, which is no small feat. So why did I tell him something so stupid? I felt like hell and sadly it didn't get better the next day either. I had fifteen new messages from Ruby, things like "I'm sorry, Adam told me you had a horrible night." "What happened, Amy?" "I have so many things to tell you, come over!"

I didn't feel like it, or honestly, I just wouldn't dare go over there and face Adam. What did he mean by "obviously head over heels for you"? Aaron? He couldn't mean himself because he had countless occasions to let me know he was interested, but he never did.

I wanted to apologize to him, but I wasn't brave enough.

I asked Ruby to come over because I needed to tidy my flat.

She was there in fifteen minutes and told me all about how much fun she'd had the evening before. She begged me not to be upset with her because she abandoned me, but she liked this new guy so much that she couldn't stop herself. She asked me to be considerate because it was the first time such a big thing had happened to her. The unexpected had happened: Ruby fell in love for the first time.

Truth to be told, I'd never seen Ruby glow like that. She'd become a completely new person, she'd totally changed. She wasn't playing the role of the ice queen anymore but the girl who could hug the whole world. I was happy to see her like that. I was secretly waiting for this kind of love too, the love that made you forget about the world and makes everything you touch more beautiful because your joy, your smile, your happiness transforms it, as it transforms you. If moments could be saved and kept forever, this is what I would like to remember, when love lifts someone up and makes them into something new.

The coming days were all about Patrick, Christian's friend. Ruby kept talking about him, every one of her sentences contained at least one mention of Patrick. Anyone else would have annoyed me, I'd have probably slapped the person, but with Ruby it was fine, she was different. I was sincerely glad to see her finally experiencing happiness.

Patrick didn't like me because that little incident with Christian cast me in the role of the bitchy friend. The girl who had a boyfriend but dated other boys. Of course, Ruby knew that the whole thing was an act, so she secretly laughed to herself when it came up between them.

I really wanted to tell her about Adam, but I just didn't have the courage. She was my best friend, she knew about everything that ever happened to me, she just couldn't know about this. I thought it better to just forget about the whole thing because it had no future, anyway. I'd hurt Adam and even if I hadn't, he didn't care about me. A newer chapter. Another boy who had kept a piece of my heart.

Summer holidays had been over for two weeks and I hadn't been to Ruby's place since the Adam mayhem, four days ago. I wanted to see him. I'd hurt him and it was eating at me. I kept thinking about him in class, I was losing my mind. I texted Violet to meet me at the sport field after History and that, if possible, she shouldn't tell Ruby. Usually all three of us participate in secret meetings like this, but I couldn't involve Ruby. I didn't want to leave her out, but Adam wasn't staying very long with them and after he'd gone, everything would be back to normal.

I hurried to the field after class because I felt that if I couldn't tell the whole story to someone right away I'd dump it all on Adam. Why couldn't he be satisfied with a tiny flame, why did he have to set a fire? It's all his fault. Why does he have to look that good and smile so sweetly? Why does he have to exist at all?

Violet had arrived earlier than me, she paced back and forth, fumbling with her hair. I didn't even have time to say hi because she interrogated me right away.

"You're not pregnant, are you?"

Considering this alternative, I was pretty lucky with just my broken heart. I'd be over it after one-two-three hundred tissues and countless tear-drenched nights.

"No, that's not what this is about."

"Huh, that's reassuring then. What's his name?"

Violet unlike Ruby, wasn't going to bite my head off, but I still found it difficult to open up to her because I didn't really know how to handle it.

"The thing is, I don't even know how, but this has happened."

"It's Adam, right? Ruby's half-brother?"

"How do you know?"

"Oh, Amy, I've seen how you two looked at each other on Friday night, before the cinema and I guess there's the reason why Ruby isn't here."

Each other? So Adam also was looking at me with unquenchable longing? I seriously doubt that.

"Please, help me! I can't stop thinking about him! If I told you that he was special, and not like all the others before him, I know you'd give me the list of all my fuckups, but I'd have to assure you that I'd fallen in love with him and I don't care if he actually isn't different, at all. I want him and only him."

Violet swore that she wouldn't tell my secret to Ruby, but she did tell me to do it myself. She thought that Ruby wouldn't mind, she was just worried that Adam would eventually hurt me, that's all. I didn't understand why Violet was thinking so far ahead since Adam didn't give a damn about me.

Thanks, Violet, I don't even know why I haven't thought of it before. I'm going to confess my feelings to both Adam and Ruby! Sure thing!

Even with Violet's very useful warning, my heart felt lighter because I could finally talk about these things with someone. I decided to forget about Adam for good and if needed, I wouldn't shy away from drastic means.

After my confession to Violet, I hurried back so I wouldn't miss my Psychology class. When I got upstairs, I heard someone cry my name twice, to make sure I hadn't gone deaf during the summer.

"Amy, Amy, stop for a minute please."

Since I wasn't trying to avoid him anymore, I managed to say hello to Aaron quite calmly.

"Listen, Amy, I know you'll say no, but I'll try nonetheless even though it's not your birthday. Would you have dinner with me on Saturday?"

I knew that under other circumstances, if I was the "old Amy" I would have given him some fake excuse, but since my talk with Adam something had changed in me. He was right in everything. Aaron had been trying hard for years to make me have dinner with him at least once in his life and I ignored him and his efforts every time. I always rejected him, hiding behind my defences, each and every time. Aaron is actually the dream guy for most girls and I'm still thinking about my answer, I must be crazy. Anyway, my agenda was to forget Adam. So the plan was easy: I had to go on a date with Aaron. That's what Adam's Saturday speech must have really meant. The new Amy was here.

"When are you picking me up?"

I could see the shock on Aaron's face as well as the happiness with himself that he'd earned a date with me, the hard way.

"Is this really a yes? I should carve it into stone that Amy Beck finally agreed to go on a date with me, on this day!"

I smiled back at him and noted to myself that I'd made a good decision, if only to see the smile that I hadn't seen on Aaron's face in such a long time. Was my smile sincere? I don't know, but it made me really happy that my small "yes" made him this excited. I also told Ruby the big news and she glowed more than Edward did when he got naked in front Bella in the sunlight. Strangely enough, agreeing to go on a date with Aaron also filled me with peace. Maybe because I knew him a bit so I knew he wasn't going to surprise me with predictable shit like "What should we see in the cinema?" Christian. I still owed Adam an apology, but I tried to reduce my thoughts about him.

# Chapter Four

Saturday night was my date with Aaron as it approached, it served as the reminder that I hadn't seen Adam for a week. Ruby never talked about Adam, it would have been difficult to squeeze him in between her tirades about Patrick.

A lot of things bothered me. My biggest problem was that going on a date with Aaron felt like a mistake. I didn't want to go out with him because I still wanted Adam, yes still. I only agreed to the dinner with Aaron because I wanted Adam to pack up and crawl out of my head. Of course, this didn't happen, Adam had already moved into my head, my heart, everywhere.

Aaron went to boot-camp for a week and I was in the clouds that I didn't need to think about our date until then. Ruby wasn't too present, being so engulfed in her romance with Patrick. Violet wasn't really around either, too busy organising the "Back to school" party. I was left alone in my frustration with desperately trying to write a new article but had no inspiration, whatsoever.

I never liked writing. Honestly, I actually hated it. In elementary school I had horrible grades on all of my essays, my spelling was catastrophic, not to mention the fact that quite often I handed in empty pages because I didn't feel like writing. I didn't feel motivated in my pursuing any of my potential as a writer until I had to write an essay about a compulsory reading. Shame or not, I hadn't read it, but based on the title I made up a whole new story. My teacher wasn't impressed and she called my parents. She told them that I had the potential to maybe end up as a great writer, but if I didn't get my act together, now I would first become a failed student. I had no intention whatsoever of becoming a writer, I wanted to be a Pop singer like every girl my age, I always pretended I was on X-factor when I was in the bathroom. I'd put the mike in my hand, the choreography in my feet and brace myself until the show started! The audience always went wild and so did my mother when during one of my "shows" I sprained my ankle. Of course, in school I told everyone that I'd fallen down the stairs, only Ruby knew the truth and I made her swear that she'd take it to her grave. After my accident, I gave upon my "singing career," especially since my performance couldn't really be labelled as singing... more like wailing. People would have paid me not to sing, and even more to stop singing.

Friday arrived and we didn't have school, so I thought about inviting Ruby to have a girly day out, but of course she'd already promised Patrick that she'd spend the whole day with him. I decided to stay home and figure out what to write about for my article. I was still rummaging through my old stuff when I heard the usual advertising-voice of a woman shouting that the audience at home, should call in right away so she could help them find true, passionate love.

*You don't say!* How can you guarantee that it's not some kind of perv' who shows up for the date? Or I don't know, a Cyclops!

"Sign up now and let the love of your life finally find you!"

That's very nice of you, but what if I've already found him, but he doesn't love me back?

However, they gave me a great idea for my next article: the advantages and disadvantages of online dating. First, however I needed to register on a dating site with a fake profile.

Dr. Love will see you now

So far, I'd only heard bad things about online dating. My friends who had tried to find love on a site like this, usually got either some F'ed up loser or a Quasimodo who posed as Antonio Banderas. I think it was sort of a punishment for them because they couldn't wait for love.

Sadly, since most guys are into blonde girls with huge boobs, I chose a girl like that to be the face of my fake profile. I tried to find someone who didn't look too easy, because I didn't want to make it obvious that my dear Melissa was only the creature of my imagination. Interests: well, I haven't quite figured out what I wanted with this whole experiment: Did I want Melissa to be swarmed by jerks or decent guys? (If they existed at all…) So, for interests: clubbing, boys, clubbing, fake boobs festivals (Okay, I didn't add the latter) While I was working hard on creating my fake persona, I got a message. My stomach started to hurt immediately because I knew Ruby wasn't going to text me at this time of the evening and what could Violet possibly want at this hour? Deep inside, I wished it was Adam with something along the lines of : "Amy Beck, I'm in love with you since I've seen you standing at the bar with that sour expression on your face. My days have no hope since you disappeared from my life." Okay, I'd actually be happy with a simple: "Hello, Stranger! How are you, it's been a long time…" Oh, well a "Hey, 'sup?" would also do and I'd sleep much better. Just please, Adam, get in touch.

I reached for my phone, but the moment I looked at the screen and saw Aaron's name, the spell broke. What did I expect? "Hey, what's up, are you home? I can't wait to see you next Saturday!" Me too, me too… and I'm not lying. Gosh, why do I need to be so negative when Aaron is such a sweet guy! I didn't hurry to answer him, but continued creating the personality of Melissa. Almost all the lines matched her "plastic doll" appearance, so I hit the sign up button.

I didn't need to wait two seconds and I already had a PM from Anaconda01:

"You're breathtakingly beautiful."

If I answered him, to go and drown yourself then, it would be very much like Amy, but now I was in the role of Melissa, so I thanked him and asked him without any prejudices what's the inspiration behind his name. I naively didn't think that it could have anything to do with the snake slithering in his pants. Accompanied by a suggestive smile, he answered this:

"If you want, I could show it to you one of these nights."

Great! I signed up five minutes ago and I've already found a pervert. I could start my article with the disadvantages. First paragraph: Beware of the pervs!

I was still Amy and thus couldn't be completely true to the personality of the made up Melissa, so I answered Anakonda01 that "I might be a snake charmer, but I'm not interested in worms."

That was it, I had no more messages from Anakonda01, his trouser snake might have been smaller than he'd wanted to believe. I continued browsing and didn't mourn him. You could say *yes* or *no* to different users and also rate them. I got hungry from all that intense hunting, so I went down to the kitchen to get some food. By the time I got back, I had a new message from "The man of your dreams." I highly doubted it. His message was so unoriginal, it hurt.

"Oh dear Juliette! (Or in this case Melissa!) I've been waiting for thousands of years to come across such a legendary beauty I could save from distress."

I could see the scene with in my mind's eyes, as Quasimodo hobbles along, winding country roads shouting "I'm coming, my princess! Hold on and I'm going to save you!"

Well, no thanks.

"Your hair is as shiny as the sun waking up the slumbering flowers!"

Slumbering flowers? What kind of simile is that?

"I'd also like to be the sun, so I may shine on you with my rays every morning."

Good gracious! I laughed so hard I almost spit my hot chocolate on the screen. I lost my way somewhere between the slumbering vegetation and the sunlight. But he kept drooling cheesiness on me through his keyboard.

"I'd write odes to you, not one, but a million, to make your days more enjoyable."

Well, surely if he keeps spouting this bullshit.

"Oh, Melissa, queen of my heart, I'd explore your lush curves like the hills of Italy."

Oh my, if there's a woman who eats up this B.S., he

deserves to explore as much as he want.

"I'm looking forward to have your speedy answer."

Keep on waiting, Don Juan!

Unfortunately, this exchange made me forget the time of the day. At least Romeo made sure I had a hilarious evening. I tried to think about what could possibly be the perfect message. It should be something you won't show to your friends, laughing. It should be something which doesn't make you feel like you ended up on the wrong planet. I think a simple "Hey, what's up?" can do the trick. It's obvious that on a dating site you message someone because you like them. Therefore, it's completely useless to tell them that you sleep with their picture at night and you never close their chat window and of course you're the guy with the huge L on your forehead.

I don't think it's a very good idea to declare our love right in the beginning because then where is the excitement? The thrill wondering if the other person is also pining away to meet you? I took a deep plunge into the basics of online dating. I'd already checked more than two-hundred home pages and I have to admit that ninety percent looked completely unfit for human reproduction, while the remaining ten percent were simply just jerks.

Susceptible jerk version one: He writes the following to the "About me" section: If you want to get to know me, do that, if not, I don't care. (*Oh, I'm Mr. Cool Cucumber*)

Susceptible jerk version two: If you're looking for the perfect man, look no further, you've found him. (*Also, if you're looking for the biggest liar*)

Version three: I'm a babe magnet! (*Yeah, that's why you had to sign up for a dating site*)

I was finally well into my article when my phone beeped. Ah, it must be Aaron, I forgot to answer the poor guy. I grabbed my phone and was about to open it when I noticed that it was sent from an unknown number. I could only see the beginning: "Hey, Amy! I hope you're not avoiding me." *It must be Adam, it can only be him! He's the only person I'm avoiding.* I opened it and it was indeed Adam. That was his message:

"Hey, Amy! I hope you're not avoiding me. You haven't come to see Ruby for a while. One of the jerks (Adam)."

What should I answer? What can I answer? I wanted to ask one of my friends for help, but I couldn't talk about it with Ruby because I was Miss Secretive and Violet was also out because I'd promised her that I'd talk to Ruby. Why are you overthinking it, Amy? Get your act together!" At times like this when I tried to calm myself, I always heard the same song in my head. I didn't know who it was by, but he had a very high-pitched voice.

"*Relax, take it easy…*"

My phone suddenly beeped again.

"I know you're home, the light is on in your house."

What? Was he camping in front of my house or what? At the same time: oh gosh, he's so sweet, I'm going to melt. But hey, how does he know I'm the one at home and not somebody else?

"Hey! No, I'm not avoiding you! I'm just busy with school stuff. How do you know I'm home?"

Hah, I wonder what he's going to say to that.

"Your light is on in your room and you've been pacing cutely back and forth since I sent you the first message.

Game over. He's won. Let's stop. No actually, I can't stop because then I'm busted. I'm looking for something, yeah, that's what I'm going to tell him.

"I'm just looking for a CD."

"Stop searching and come down to have a burger with me!"

It's starting again: the nervousness, the knot in my stomach and I can't help it because I want to see him, I must see him.

I looked out of the window and I saw him standing there with his hands in his pockets, with his usual Adam-charm; he looked a bit sleepy, but very handsome. He grinned and told me he'd wait for me there. I didn't remember agreeing, but if he'd decided for me, I didn't mind. If I hadn't known that he was waiting for me downstairs, I would have jumped up and down on my bed, but I had to keep my cool. I put on my jeans and a coral red top and ran down the stairs. I came to a halt before opening the door and took a deep breath so that he wouldn't figure out I was hopping down the stairs like a hyperactive mountain goat.

Adam stood by our fence in the exact same pose I saw him from above. From his lips, all the extra cheesy flowery-sunshiny bullshit, that I couldn't tolerate from other guys, would sound like sweet confessions to my ravenous crush.

"Aren't you going to be cold?"

"No, I'm going to be fine, it's pretty mild for September."

If I'm cold, I'll just ask for your jumper and elegantly forget to give it back, and then during the night I'll perform some kind of magical rite with it, to bind you to myself until the end of my life or until I fall out of love with you.

"Alright, Amy Beck! Tell me why you disappeared, if you're not avoiding me!"

Okay, this was my opportunity, my big chance to ask for his forgiveness and confess my true feelings for him. Of course, I only got as far as saying sorry.

"Look, Adam, I want to say sorry for last time. I didn't want to hurt you and you were right in so many things."

"Let's forget about it, okay?"

"I was really rude and I'm sorry, I don't know what got into me."

"Chill, Amy, I'm not angry with you anymore, I couldn't be, even if I wanted to."

Oh, so I get special treatment! I hope he doesn't consider me to be some silly younger sister or something like that. That'd be the worst!

"Okay , so what should we eat then? The usual stuff?"

"Yeah, for you only meat- I remembered! I'll eat the usual stuff with everything."

On the way, I told Adam about my new article and about the means I had to take to write it. He had a good laugh, especially at the expense of Romeo. We wondered if he talked like that in real life too. Adam improvised in Romeo's role:

"Dearest Amy, your carriage is ready. After your rosy cheeks are rested from your beauty sleep, I would like to invite your Highness for dinner."

"Oh, dear Adam, I would like to graciously thank your most kind invitation, I am more than glad to oblige. I'll wear my most beautiful ball gown and I will be on pins and needles, waiting for your carriage to arrive."

"When the second hand rushed past the fiftieth minute, I shall be there for you and even wait for you if necessary. But only until the burger place is open."

"When the clock has struck its last minute, I shall wait for your arrival at the gate."

We broke out laughing and even exchanged a look because we dared to mock the amorous letter of this poor corny guy, whom, if we want to be completely honest, wasn't even that funny. Adam was so incredibly cool. He was just like me, in a male version. *I know who said I was cool? Let's just say that we really got each other.* It was so good to hear his voice again and to smell his special Adam smell. He must have some special cologne for these occasions, probably called "Girl Romancer." It's just like his smile. Your legs open up by themselves, even before your brain sent an order to them.

I felt exactly the same as last time with him: the tingling sensation that I don't want our walk to be over, I don't want him to be far from me. His proximity relaxed me. I knew that if we were attacked by a ginormous dinosaur horde, he wouldn't push me under their feet, so he'd have more time to run, but he'd softly take my hand and whisper the obvious truth in my ears: "We're done for in a few minutes." I would die happily with him next to me.

Time flew by without me being able to stop it. I wanted to stay in the moment when we were walking half way. Adam more or less told me about the reason for his lingering, but I pushed him on about it, until I had the whole story. I was getting suspicious that maybe he worked undercover for the C.I.A. He assured me that he was working on his book. Well, well!

I tried to get him to spill the beans, about whatever he was writing, but he told me that he had to keep it a secret for the moment, but I would know everything when the time came.

My curiosity was killing me, I could actually feel his pangs every time I asked him a question. I've heard all about the proverbial cat killed by curiosity, but I didn't worry too much.

On the way back, it seemed that both of us were trying to walk a bit slower, but maybe I was the only one moving at the speed of a snail. The temperature dropped from one moment to the other, but I didn't dare ask for his jumper. I didn't even want him to see that I was cold because it would have netted me the "I've told you so" monologue.

We talked about Ruby, telling me that she's spending all her time with that Patrick guy. To quote him verbatim: "that chicken brain managed to make our Ruby fall completely head over heels for him." It reassured me to know that I'm not the only one disliking that dumbass. I was in the middle of complaining about Patrick when I stumbled on a pebble. *Well, I should really write,* a *small rock, then I might seem like less of a loser when I read it back.* That pebble, or small rock, was surely not there before I stumbled on it. I'm there grumbling and boom! I think I'll try to complain a bit less from now on, before I fall another time. Adam was of course having a great time with my accident. First the little hypocrite asked me if I was alright, then he burst out laughing. Laughing dimples appeared on his face and I decided to stay on the ground a little bit longer, otherwise I would melt in his arms.

I could have died and he's laughing at me! And how could I be alright, braniac? If you hadn't noticed, and I guess you hadn't, I'm head over heels for you and this is the most embarrassing thing that could have happened to me.

He pulled me up with a nonchalant superhero move and he put his furry, blue jumper on my shoulders. I could have tried to refuse it, but I had no power against him. Not to mention the fact that I had absolutely no intention of taking it off. The jumper was a perfect fit for me, just like Adam. His jumper smelled exactly like him. The smell that's going to haunt me for a while, the smell that is always going to remind me of him and the smell I will want to find on every and any guy from now on.

"Yes, you could've surely break your neck on that tiny

pebble. Should I call an ambulance? Have you broken your leg?"

"Okay, keep mocking me, please!"

I thanked him for helping me up and we walked on. A girl always hopes that a moment like this starts something between us and that the other person feels the same thing you do. Suddenly Adam broke the silence which I thought was romantic, with a sentence as far from romantic as you can possibly get.

"Next week I'm going on a date."

What? A date? You are going on a date and not We? A lump formed in my throat and my eyes teared up, but I tried to hold them back with a sigh. He couldn't see it, he couldn't know it. Inside my fragile thought bubble, a scene fit for Dirty Dancing, wherein I jump into Adam's arms on a quiet meadow popped, violently. I didn't know what to think. I just didn't get what was going on. Why did he ask me to go out to have a burger with him and trying to be friendly with me then?

I wanted to push him into the pond in the middle of the island, but I managed to squeeze out an answer.

"I'm glad to hear that."

It sounded stupid especially since it must've been written on my face that I thought the exact opposite. *Chill, Amy, you're home in twelve minutes, then you can cry as much as you want.*

"Ruby told me that next week you're having a date with the local heartthrob, Aaron or whatever that kid is called."

Kid? Because you're such an adult, right? You invite me to get a burger twice, you create thousands of romantic scenes in my head then you let me down. Congrats! What a mature man! Why do you even care, anyway? Mind your own business and love life!

"Yeah, Aaron is a very nice guy."

*What do I care about him being nice, if he's not the one I want.* The lump in my throat didn't want to disappear and I needed to pull myself together so I didn't answer him with a shaking voice. He didn't seem very happy either. After a few sentences we both looked like people going through a breakup or something. He walked me home, but I didn't really understand why. We stopped at the gate for a few minutes and I shyly searched his eyes. I didn't want him to notice that inside, I felt awful because he was going on a date with someone else. His eyes shined and I sort of expected him to kiss me to give the evening a happy end. Of course, nothing happened. We stared at each other for long moments, then he leaned closer and planted a kiss on my forehead.

I read in a silly women's magazine when I was younger, that a kiss on the forehead is very humiliating. It was true. He'd told me that he was seeing someone, then he came with this forehead kiss nonsense then the end, he walked away. I stared after him, sort of expecting him to come back to tell me that he'd been kidding, there was no other girl, or just to comeback and kiss me. If my feelings were true, it's what should happen, isn't it?

He left without ever looking back. My heart broke. I collapsed on our porch and cried. I was wiping away my tears when I realised that I was still wearing his jumper. I went inside tore it off and threw it on top of the heap of dirty clothes in the middle of my room.

Unfortunately, I must have been wearing it too long because I smelt his smell for the rest of the evening. I hated it, I hated Adam and the girl he was going to see and who wasn't me. Maybe Aaron is really the one for me, he would never leave me and he would appreciate me. Adam dumped me before we even got together. I don't need all that drama, crying every night. That's not how it should be.

My mood swings tormented me all night long. By the time I convinced myself that Aaron was the right one, Adam had already wormed his way into my head with his smooth face, inviting me to a burger, with his treacherous niceness as he gave me his jumper. I hated Adam again.

That was my whole weekend. I refused to communicate with anyone, but my mum. Ruby tried to reach out, but I told her that I was ill and since she still had Patrick-fever, she didn't notice I'd fed her a white lie.

I spent most of my weekend with mum, we held a cheer-up afternoon, watched like ten romantic comedies, we stuffed our face with sweets and I told her everything.

They just came back from their summer holidays. They usually leave in the last week of August, so their return usually falls in early September. This year, since they considered me an adult, they allowed me to skip the family holiday. Of course, only if we talked on the phone every day. I'd missed mum a lot. I enjoyed being with her because she talked like a romantic heroine. She believed that it didn't matter how many times a boy walked out of your life because if he came back once, then he always would. There were some complicated fates. Sometimes your story couldn't be simple because you had to fight for each other to be happy in the end. But how can you know if the other feels the same?

Mum had an answer for this as well, like she did for everything, but this time it didn't help me.

There was no good answer to this question. You can't predict who your husband will be plus the feelings of the other person is also a mystery. You should feel it inside, that he belongs to you. It doesn't matter how many times you ran in circles or how you found your way back to each other, because in the end all that matters is that you manage to get back to the beginning.

Alright, alright. It's all very beautiful, but I want Adam today, maybe tomorrow, but not in years from now! Anyway, it wouldn't be the same then! Mum had another favourite saying which drove me mad:

"Don't run after a car that doesn't stop to pick you up."

That is: Why don't you understand, sweet child of mine, that this boy doesn't give a hoot about you?

But Adam's proverbial car has already taken me out to have a burger with him. So, you tell me, Mother of all, what does that mean?

Mum just laughed and held me tight. Her comforting hugs also worked their magic on me, so I felt a lot better by Sunday night. I postponed finishing my article and let the homework wait until my heart healed. Started to read a self-help book I'd snitched from my mum's shelf, but I never found the occasion to actually read it.

By the first page I was immediately informed that I was wonderful. "It doesn't matter what others say, you should always know that you're wonderful!" It's nice, but it smells a bit of bullshit, doesn't it? Of course, one should always feel that one is wonderful, but there are always periods in one's life when one just can't feel that way: like now. If I was so wonderful, why didn't Adam want me?

I abandoned the book at the same place, just like last time: Chapter 1/ Part 1: "Everything happens as it should happen." *No, no, no! I have to disagree! I think Adam and I should be together and if the universe thinks differently, then the universe is wrong!*

It was around eight pm, when I got a text. I didn't feel like reading it, so I ignored it. I was leaving my room, when my phone rang like crazy. Somebody wasn't giving up. If it was Adam, well then, he was too late. If it was Aaron, I'd find some sort of good excuse. My curiosity got the better of me. It was Ruby: "Call me back, please, it's over!"

Over? What's over?

# Chapter Five

I suddenly understood. I hit the call back button right away so I could talk to Ruby as soon as possible. She was crying when she answered. She tried to fill me in on the details, fighting her tears and I did my best to piece together the puzzle of what happened.

"He chea-cheated on me, that, that pig!"

Yeah, I got that he was a pig without repetition. She was talking about Patrick, who else? Suddenly, I didn't care about my own heartbreak or the fact that I might run into Adam if I ran over to her flat. Judging from her voice, I guessed that she cried her eyes out, so she was in no condition to come to my place. I told mum that it was a Ruby S.O.S and in the next moment I was already in my coat, looking for my shoes. I managed to fish them out from among all the others then I was on my way to Ruby's. Once I arrived at her house, the next thing I saw was Adam and some girl. *The girl*, to be exact. The girl I loathed and whose name was Cassie.

Cassie's story: she was born at the same time as us, so sadly her presence haunted our school years. She was everybody's friend and nobody's friend. She always gossiped about the people who weren't present, she wasn't two-faced, she was literally a-thousand-faced. There were no boys who would be taboo for her. We were around twelve when she learnt that I liked a boy called Jake, so she wrote him a letter about how much in love I was with him, just because I was too shy to tell it to him myself. It was so embarrassing! From that moment on Jake looked at me as if I was some kind of crazy fangirl, even though I wasn't that into him. Getting back to Cassie, nobody liked her, even boys despised her because

51

of her behaviour. Later everyone learnt that Cassie was a grandmaster of intrigue.

She stood there with Adam, leaning against the fence. I felt horrible, I couldn't believe that Adam wanted Cassie of all people? Why? He could have chosen anyone but her. I grunted a "hello" to them, then hurried past them. Ruby was waiting for me in the door and jumped on my neck. I think both of us needed that hug. I didn't want to let Ruby go because I felt like my world had stopped existing with Adam's. We went up to her room where she told me about what happened with Patrick in a disturbingly calm voice.

She'd found out that Patrick had been in a "happy" relationship for three years, a fact he'd forgotten to share with poor Ruby. Rage fogged up my vision. How could someone be such an asshole? Ruby didn't care. She said that she refused to cry for more than half an hour over some guy. That interval had just ran out, right then, so it was now all in the past. Ruby was back to her Cruelle de Ville self, and I loved her this way, with her stone-cold heart. Why can't I be like her? Why can't I just ignore Adam? I didn't have to worry about Ruby, but there was plenty to worry about myself. To change subject to a fresh bit of gossip, she started complaining about Adam and Cassie.

"You've also seen them all tangled up at the gate, that girl makes me sick!"

I don't know if it was from hearing the word "tangled up" or imagining Adam kissing that monster, but I just couldn't hold back anymore. I cried like a baby. Ruby put her arms around me, although she had no idea what happened to me.

"Did I say something wrong? I can promise not to say anything wrong about them if it provokes such a reaction."

I think the time has come to…

"No, Ruby, that's not it. But we have to talk."

She studied my face, frowning, trying to riddle out what's suddenly got into me. I tried to stop my heart from beating in my throat so I'd be able to finally tell her the truth that was so obvious. Amy, the time has come, said the annoyingly self-important voice in my head which always guides me towards the not always easy, but right path. I covered my face with my hands and I let the following words leave my mouth.

"I'm in love with Adam."

I pulled my two pinkie fingers away and I tried to scout out Ruby's reaction while I felt my heart slowly beating slower. I didn't feel like I'd suffocate right away or that I'd pass out and my life would be over. I felt lighter. No matter what Ruby would say, I already felt relieved. For a moment Ruby sat in silence then put her hand on mine and pulled it away from my face.

"You really think I didn't know?"

She knew, and she let me suffer in silence when it was obvious that it was killing me!

"Why didn't you say anything?"

"You're my best friend, so naturally, I thought you'd tell me whenever you felt like it. I've only known Adam's version of events, and while we're at it, I'm hurt that you didn't tell me anything."

Adam's version? Does he have his own version?

"What would you have said if I told you that yet again, I'd managed to fall for someone you cautioned me to keep away from?

I didn't get it. If it had been this easy all along to tell Ruby, then I could've confessed my horrible sin already. Anyway, I wasn't prepared to fall in love with Adam, I'd say the attraction I felt for him hit me like a lightening bolt.

"Amy, you're my best friend, for heaven's sake. If you do good things or bad things, if you fall for the right guy or the wrong one, I'm going to be by your side no matter what. We've always known about each other's missteps. Do you get it? Always! It scared me that you didn't dare to talk to me about Adam. I don't think I ever gave you a reason to not trust me, did I?"

This was the moment when I had to look inside myself. Ruby was completely right. We've been through so much shit together. She wasn't just my best friend, she was my other half, the one I could trust with all of my secrets. Even if it was about a dead body buried in my back yard. Well, I'd have to bury Ruby next to the body, because a secret is only a secret if only one person knows it. If two people know about it, one of them might gossip. But she really knew me I had to give her that. She knew my life, my biggest secrets, everything. I had to apologise. Not tomorrow, not after that, but this instant.

"I'm sorry I've been so stupid! I don't know what came over me, I believed that I was a grown-up who could hold her love life in check, but I was wrong. I'd spent hours looking at guys online, hoping that someone would keep me from thinking of your merboy of a half-brother, but it didn't happen."

Ruby didn't say anything, and I knew why. She was hurt because for the first time in our friendship, she didn't know something about me. For me, however, it was nice to know that someone was paying this much attention to me. There weren't many people in one's life who knew us this well, who knew our secrets, or fears and desires, things we'd hardly dare to confess to ourselves. Ruby was like this for me. If one could wish for a friend, it should be like Ruby.

"You don't have to apologise for anything. Just please, trust me next time! I don't care if it's Adam or someone else, but please don't feel like I'm going to bite your head off or despise you because I won't. I love you and I respect your decisions, I'll just fulfil my duty as a friend to warn you if you're doing something stupid. That's what makes me your friend, the fact that I'm not assisting you with doing anything stupid just like you won't let me do anything ridiculous either. That's why our friendship is honest and true."

I didn't say anything because my tears kept falling, I hugged Ruby and the only thing I could think of was how lucky I was for having her. There could be any boy, the love of my life, romance, crush, fire or just a little spark, I don't care what's going to happen, if they stay or go because I'll always have Ruby. Some teardrops glistened in Ruby's eyes, but she made a joke out of it —she didn't understand why she didn't kick Patrick out before, like after their first date.

I related the whole Adam story to her, from my point of view. The only thing a boy says about a perfect date is something like "Ah, she was cute and we had a great time." While the girl depicts the first date down to the smallest detail: "Then we stepped out of the gate, and the gate was just as green as his eyes, then he gave me that look… then this and this happened in this and that moment."

Oh well, every story has a "girl version" and a "boy version." Ruby didn't get Adam either, who, apparently, asked or talked about me twenty-two hours out of the twenty-four. While claiming that he didn't care about me, he was just curious. Ruby saw through him, just as she saw through me. Ruby enlightened me that Adam only asked Cassie out after he'd learned about Aaron. She only told Adam about my date because she wanted to see what reaction the news would provoke in him. I didn't really know what to do with the new information because Adam must have known that I had feelings for him and if he whistled, I'd run to him. Okay, it wouldn't have hurt if he had fought for me a bit, but honestly it would've been enough if he simply opened his mouth and told me about his feelings, if he really had any, that is. The whole thing was like some F'ed up romantic comedy. Because of our own stupidity, we dated everyone but each other. Couldn't it all be so easy. Why wouldn't it? This was only Ruby's point of view though.

I had a very different opinion: if we're interested in someone, then we fight for them, we don't give up and we don't go on dates with other people. Of course, we had to disregard the fact that I'm going on a date with Aaron to forget about Adam because I knew what I was doing and why. I stayed for an hour then I went home. Fortunately, Adam & Co. weren't at the gate when I got there. My heart beat as quickly as it did when I'd first seen them, but something had changed: now I knew that I had Ruby. Everything was much easier to bear now, with Ruby on my side. Aaron was still up in the air, with his approaching return. I looked forward to our date and at the same time I didn't. I still held out hope that he'd be able to keep my thoughts from Adam, but I knew the chances for this were nearing zero. Ruby thought that the wonderful merboy only dated Cassie because I also had a date.

55

This absurd childish revenge was just too much, even from him!

I felt guilty because I still hadn't answered Aaron's last message, so I quickly sent him an apologetic text and also told him that I was looking forward to our date. Okay, it wasn't very nice of me that the second half of my text was a little white lie. He answered within two seconds. I got home and fell into bed still in my day clothes. My thoughts raced and I couldn't decide what was a good idea and what wasn't. Maybe I just needed to be alone to purge the chaos from my head and from my life. I concluded that if I spent as much time concentrating on school as I did with my lame love life, I'd be top of the class. Nevertheless, I didn't want to go to school the next day, I rather stay home with my sadness and avoid Cassie's victorious owl-face.

Despite all of that, I still tried to get into the mood for my Saturday night date. In my head I made up an Adam and an Aaron list. Let's see what they have in common with me. Adam and I both hate when someone blocks our way when we're getting off public transportation. Okay, one tick. We like writing. We have the same favourite breakfast cereal. It was my favourite first, but who cares. He's also scared of roller coasters. To be more exact, he's scared that it might collapse when he's on it. I understood him because I've been terrified of that thought since I was a child. He's also stepped into dog poop and then hoped the whole day long that it would bring him luck, but it didn't. His favourite animated show's also Courage, the cowardly dog. He often watched foreign series hoping that he'd pick up a language this way and that's how he learnt Italian and Spanish... and this is how I've learnt...uhm. Nothing. Yet! But I'm working on it. Oh, well, this one is just half a tick then. He can only fall asleep if his feet are carefully tucked in under the blanket thus minimising the chance of something biting them off during the night. I remember him laughing like hell, telling me that I probably have such small feet because they stuck out from under my blanket when I was a small child and something must have munched on them. Just like me, he only likes lemon ice tea, rejecting the peach flavour totally. He can only bear it once a year tops, and only if It's some emergency. He's left-handed, just like me. (That's quite rare, let's admit it.) He likes to fall asleep with the TV on (me too, although my parents aren't that happy with it because they need to turn it off for me.) We have so many things in common! How can he not see it?

Okay let's see about Aaron. Well. We go to the same school. Tick. We lost our kiss-virginity at the same time… with each other. He has a brown jumper. Me too. He also fell asleep during Maths class and had to stay after school until five as a punishment. It's happened to me too. He has a dog. Well, it's not really a common trait because I have a tiny dog, Snowflake, a bichon Bolognese. Aaron actually doesn't have a dog but he might have had one at one point in his life, or he will have one and then I can add it to the list. Anyway, Snowflake was a tiny, cute dog only for me, for everybody else he was a real beast.

I should haves slept, but I couldn't and there was nothing interesting in the TV either, only boring commercials. In the morning I looked just as shitty as I felt. I was afraid of the look Cassie would give me, although she didn't know I liked Adam, so she shouldn't feel obliged to tell me about their date, but knowing her, she surely would.

Ruby waited for me in front of our house and we went to school together. Fortunately, it wasn't very far, just a fifteen minute walk Ruby tried to use to cheer me up, with no success. I wanted the whole thing to be over. I wanted to know if they'd become a couple so I could let the whole thing go.

We also picked up Violet on our way and for the first time in a long time I didn't need to avoid answering questions. Ruby and Violet discussed the school party which was in two weeks. I wanted to have the whole Aaron thing behind me too, and really everything. To be honest, I really wished for a cloak of invisibility, so I could wear it for the rest of my life.

Reaching the school everyone walked a bit more briskly, hurrying to get to their class, except for us who still walked in our leisurely pace, but we still got into school five minutes before eight. Sadly, this five minutes was enough for the owl-faced Cassie, who was perching on her desk, to tell us about her fabulous night.

"Why didn't we come in late?" I whispered to Ruby. We'd managed to miss the beginning, but we had plenty of time to hear how the story ended.

"Oh, this boy kissed me so softly that my whole body became Jell-O."

I'll give you such a kiss that all your teeth fall out. The only person Adam can kiss is me! He tainted our love by dating a frog like Cassie!

Ruby squeezed my hand when Cassie greeted us, "Well Ruby, to be more exact."

"Hey, Sister-in-law!"

Luckily, Ruby wasn't to be intimidated by stupid frogs.

"Sister-in-law! How sweet! You're about the one hundred twentieth girl, who called me that. It'll stick with someone eventually!"

Cassie's face went so red that I thought she would explode. Ruby sat down in the back, ignoring Cassie's hurt expression and started talking about the weekend. Ruby's reaction saved me, and the whole class, from listening to Cassie's blown up story all day long. Well, this was over at least.

They kissed. So what. *I should forget him already!*

My day went by without any major events. I couldn't concentrate in class because I always caught myself imaging that I was walking hand in hand with Adam. Somewhere in another world, another dimension, but at least I was happy. When my happy bubble was popped, I saw Cassie and Adam walking hand in hand. I also saw myself sneaking up behind them, kicking out Cassie's foot from under her, then I jumped in Adam's arms and we lived happily ever after, until Cassie comes around and takes her revenge. School was over soon, we had only four classes that day and the whole week was pretty relaxed. I got lost in the whirlpool of days and my only wish was for the week to be over. Ruby tried to invite me over every day, but I always refused. I didn't have the feeling that I

58

wanted to see Adam, my reason for it was quite simple: I didn't want to see him. He was the last person I wished to see, alongside Cassie of course. I asked Ruby not to say anything about him in order to forget him as quickly as possible. Ruby complied, she didn't even mention him when I was around.

Saturday night was drawing dangerously near and we agreed with Aaron when he would come to pick me up.

I spent Friday night at home with Ruby, we watched movies. She told me that Patrick came to see her recently and begged her to take him back. Luckily, she had her wits around, not like me. She wouldn't fall into the same pit twice. Me, on the other hand... If there was a huge billboard in the middle of the road saying "Attention! Your heart will be broken again if you enter!" I would happily waltz in. Because why not? A billboard couldn't possibly know what would happen to me. Ruby, of course, would be cleverer than me.

She was more excited about the date with Aaron than I was. He was supposed to pick me up at seven and take me out for dinner to one of the best restaurants in town, the Carthago. The perfect restaurant, the perfect evening, the perfect guy, the perfect date. That's how I could describe things with Aaron, everything is always so damn perfect with him. No question marks, no doubts if he was tricking me, he sure made life easier.

I straightened my hair and put on a sort of minidress because mum taught me that I shouldn't show too much of myself on the first date because then there'd be no second date just one night to draw consequences from. Aaron was a gentleman in this respect as well, if I opened my legs to him, he would kindly refuse. In any case I decided on a not too provocative outfit (well, sort of not too provocative.)

Aaron parked his car in front of our house at seven sharp. I was excited, but not so much about the date, more so about the successfulness of this mission to hopefully make me forget Adam. If Aaron couldn't make me forget Adam, this stupid crush would plague my life because I couldn't find a boy more perfect than Aaron. He kissed me on the cheek and opened the car's door for me.

Hah, that stupid ass Christian never even got out of his damned car to open my door. Aaron was a true gentleman. On the way there we talked about school, our respective classmates and I asked him if he was willing to be interviewed for my article about heartthrobs. He laughed and agreed. Shyly, but with his usual Aaron-like nonchalance he added that he may be the heartthrob of the school but his heart had been taken for years. His eyes were pinned to the road, but he gave me a quick glance. I understood right away that he was talking about me. Why didn't I ever take his advances seriously? Was it all too incredible to believe that someone like him wanted me? That there was someone who really only wanted me?

We arrived in front of the Carthago. Aaron parked his car and I waited for him at the entrance. A lot of students from our school came here, this was a popular place for couples, the place where boys brought the girl of their dreams. I spotted multiple members of his fan club as we walked in, side by side and I knew they would curse me for the rest of my life if I didn't leave Aaron for them as a dessert. *Don't worry girls, I've been cursed since my birth so adding your curses to the cauldron wouldn't make much of a difference.*

During dinner we discussed our lives, we also talked about Ruby, Cassie and Violet. It was nice to be with Aaron, like being with an old friend, trying to share memories from the past ten years. We went for a little walk after dinner. It was the same walk but with a different boy, different feelings. I knew he was the perfect guy, the boy who would do everything for me. Yet something was missing.

There are three types of boys a girl can meet. The first one makes her believe that everything's her fault and she'll never be good enough for anybody. The second one would do anything for her, but she's just not that into him. And the third type who's not perfect, who doesn't show up like a fairy tale prince, he only arrives when you already gave up on him. With him even the imperfect becomes perfect and she gives her heart to him without fear.

Aaron was a type two kind of guy. As we walked a feeling

grew inside of me: I wanted to be with Adam. Maybe it was the biggest mistake of my life, but I didn't care. During the whole walk Aaron was waiting for the right moment to kiss me, I knew it because girls feel these kinds of things. I also wanted that kiss because it was my last chance for the fireworks and to stop longing for Adam and long for Aaron instead. We were strolling alongside the river bank when Aaron told me he wanted to ask me something.

"Amy, it's very hard for me although I've been preparing to do this for years."

*Oh, no, it already started off badly. God, please, don't say you're in love with me or I'll jump off a bridge.* He continued in a slightly trembling voice.

"I've been in love with you ever since I kissed you in the history camp."

*Where's that bridge? Or a rope, or anything I could wrap around my neck to bid goodbye to this cruel world?* Why doesn't it work with Aaron? Why? I'd really like it, but... "But" always ruins things. Aaron should be the perfect man for me, not Adam. I could've torn my own hair out when I thought this. I wanted a decent guy who was there for me. Who was there for me and also in love with me, but I didn't actually want the nice guy. I wanted the jerk who was full of question marks. Sure, Amy, walk into his trap again. Fortunately, Aaron couldn't see into my head, so he continued his confession, ignorant of the turmoil in my mind.

"And I've wanted to kiss you ever since."

After finishing his sentence, he slowly leaned closer to my lips. I didn't want to ruin his moment, the minute he'd been waiting for heaven knows since when. I was the only one who knew this moment was a lie, but I owed him this much, a kiss. His kiss was sweet, just like I remembered, but it was nothing like when I was with Adam. He hugged me afterwards and before I started worrying about going to hell for this, I heard Cassie's voice behind my back.

I turned and could hardly breathe; Cassie was standing there with Adam. The Adam I thought about when Aaron kissed me. *Funny.* So, Adam must have seen the whole thing, he saw me being with someone else, kissing someone else. But that's what he wanted, isn't it? He was the one encouraging me to notice what was before my eyes all along. Then why does it feel like cheating on him? Why does he look at me as if I've cheated on him? Cassie greeted us as if we were her old friends.

I felt embarrassed. I hated the whole situation, and I hated myself for being so insensitive. It wasn't fair to Aaron, or to anyone actually. I lied to him, I lied to myself. *Why force it? Why try it?* Love isn't like this, it's not something that slowly appears after a while, like something that had been there all along.

# Chapter Six

We said hello to Adam and Cassie and I poked Aaron, urging him to leave. Adam's expression would haunt me for a while, I was sure. Aaron had football training Sunday morning, so I suggested that we should go home so that he could have his rest. He insisted on driving me home and I didn't protest because he'd have thought I was crazy. He walked me to my door and when we stopped he turned me to face him.

"Amy, I don't know what that kiss meant for you, but it meant the world to me."

I smiled at him idiotically, but I couldn't say anything. *Please, don't say this, it just makes me feel even more horrible.* I know I should feel something... something, but it was nothing compared to what I felt when Adam gave me his jumper. Aaron gave me a goodnight kiss then went home. I sat on the porch for about ten minutes to gather my strength to go into the house and face the side of me which momentarily made me sick.

"Amy!"

What the hell?

"Adam? What are you doing here?"

*And the more important question: where did you leave that bitch?* Of course, I kept this jealous question to myself.

"That's how you imagined it?"

What is he talking about? What did I imagine how?

"I don't know what you're talking about."

"The kiss. That's how you'd imagined it?"

I could ask him his favourite question: "So should I say something?"

63

"I hadn't thought about it before."

His eyes sparkled, then he held my face firmly and kissed me on the lips. My legs trembled. My whole body melted from that one kiss.

"Did you feel this when Aaron kissed you?"

"And did you feel this when you kissed Cassie?"

I pushed him away and went into the house without any further comments.

I was fed up with him. *Who does he think he is? Whenever he feels like it, he just comes to my house to kiss me while he's dating another girl. Not to mention the fact that he follows me home just because he's seen me with Aaron?*

I went up to my room and started throwing my clothes from the floor into the wardrobe. I don't know what it was good for, but it helped me calm down a bit. My phone vibrated; I got a text.

I didn't care what Mr. "Today I want you" had to say. He surely had a good explanation for this whole thing too. I guess he didn't care about Cassie and if I hadn't pushed him away, maybe we'd have lived happily ever after. Well, until one of us messed up.

I thought about his kiss all night long. This was the only kiss in my life that almost killed me, it bound me to him it was the kiss I'd been waiting for so long.

Then I thought about Aaron. What would I tell him? Sorry but you're too nice for me so just drop it? Although it's pretty close to the truth; he is too nice for me.

I don't even deserve him. Aaron should be with a girl, who's not a crazy goose pining away after a dubious jerk, but for the guy who really loved her. Yes, Aaron should be with a nice girl because he deserves it. What do I deserve? A big slap in the face, maybe two. I should tell Aaron what's going on, not right away of course, after all it was past midnight, but sometime in the near future. Let's say tomorrow or the day after tomorrow, or the day after that, or maybe I should just hope that he'll figure it out by himself. No, I can't do that to him.

It's so messed up. Why am I doing this? I want Adam

that's clearer than day light. I don't know when this whole thing started; when him and I became us. It might have been the very moment I met him. To be honest, it might have been even before that. We were given a chance to live in the moment or to F' it up. You know what? I won't be a coward, I won't be afraid, I won't be tormented by the doubt of whether or not he is going to stay by my side. I want to cease the opportunity to be happy, not one day in the future, but right now. I have to go after him. Who cares about bitchy Cassie or the fact that I think Adam is a jerk for going on a date with her? I want him and I know he wants me. Our meeting was destined and it's not a coincidence that he makes me feel like I've found my home. My brain has lied to me, but my heart hasn't and for a while it was only pointing in his direction.

I was still dressed up, so I just had to put on my coat and run after him. I didn't find him in front of our house, although I'd secretly hoped he would be there. Nothing could stop me from telling him that I was hopelessly in love with him and for him I would tear out all of Cassie's hair if that's what he needed. I hoped he needed nothing of that sort. He should choose me without further ado, but if he had reservations, I'd tell him that I was willing to fight for him. Wow, how romantic! A girl who is willing to fight for their beloved boy. I started running because I knew all too well that if I kept on thinking about these things I would turn back. By the time I got half way I was repeating my confession like a mantra.

"Adam, I don't know where to begin, but I'll start anyway.

I know I'd only say silly things if I wanted to make an elaborate speech and of course it's not a text I've made up and memorised on the way here, but well, the thing is, I'm in love with you. Don't ask, I don't understand how it could have happened either."

As I got closer to Ruby's house, words started to fail me. By the end of my monologue, I was just at the point of telling him the first thing that came to my mind, like "Hey, you! I have feelings for you." Or maybe I shouldn't say anything other than, I was accidentally in the neighbourhood.

Great, I think it's best if I turn back. Right now! No, Amy, chill. Get your ass to Adam, it's only a few minutes more and you're there. Only five minutes, now just four, three, only two...

When we love someone with the ardour of young girls or if we're smitten with them, then one tiny moment is enough for our dream-world to burn to the ground. After that point, we won't be the same ever again, because our first disappointment kills those childish dreams, like when we believe that something could last forever.

I first met this feeling when I was with Dylan. I never thought I'd ever feel the same, but of course I was wrong. I was around the corner from Ruby's house when I saw Adam and Cassie. They stood there together and I wished I could stop existing. I really wanted Adam, but I realised I had to understand something, this above all other things. I'd never seen Adam happy with Cassie. He'd never smiled at her the way he smiled at me. His behaviour had changed with her. I had to understand that the face he was wearing now was only one from the numerous others I'd seen before. The smiles he gave me weren't for me, but for the moment. I was wrong. I wasn't special for him. I could hate him, but I was unable to do so. I loved him and this might have been the first real moment when I dared to admit this to myself without any denial. I loved him and I had to accept that it was pointless, because he didn't love me back. I had to let him go even if it meant letting go of a part of my heart.

I turned around and went home. I wasn't sad, although it would have made me feel better to see him because at that moment I didn't feel anything. I couldn't even cry. I wanted to continue my life the way it was before I met him. Without him.

I had a text from Adam on my phone, but I didn't open it. I deleted it, just like I deleted him. From everywhere. I was dragging myself home, devoid of any possibility for happiness, until I got another text. *Why can't he just leave me alone? Why does he keep texting me?*

I wanted to delete it when I saw it was from Aaron.

"Hey, Amy! I don't even know where to begin."

*It starts like a break-up message!* I kept on reading.

"I had a great time with you tonight."

I could feel a ginormous but coming up, the damned but I've talked about before.

"But…"

Haven't I told you that there was a "but" coming up?

"The thing is, that I didn't get the impression that you felt the same way as I did. I'd be the happiest guy on earth if you answered that you were just tired or stressed out by school, but I think it's something different. Whatever you tell me, I'll accept it. XOXO, Aaron."

If I was even a tiny bit interested in him, I'd probably panic that I must have been a horrible kisser and that's how he wanted to get rid of me, but in my current predicament I didn't really care about reasons. How could Aaron figure it out? God, I hope I didn't accidentally call him Adam. I owe him the truth, especially if I lied it would only lead to new lies or even worse, a new date.

"Look, Aaron! I know this must be the lamest text in the history of humankind, but I owe you the truth. You're a super nice guy, probably the nicest guy I know. I could make up a lot of better answers, but I don't want to. I'm in love with someone else.I didn't mean to lead you on, I just wanted to give it a go and I'm terribly sorry that it turned out this way."

How could I write so much bullshit? I hoped he would be able to forgive me one day and then we'd be back to where we were initially. Even if it wasn't the exactly same, I hoped it could be something similar, that we'd stay friends and we wouldn't mess that up because we both knew it couldn't be more than that.

I felt awful, but at least the chaos in my head was gone. I didn't want anything else, but to be alone. I could've ran to Ruby, but I didn't want to. I didn't need consolation, I needed time alone. My soul would calm down with time, because despite everything, I still believed. I believed that there was someone, somewhere who thought I was worthy of love.

Someone who could love me as I was. Someone who would give me their jumper, someone who would wait for me to get up if I stumbled on a pebble. He would wait for me to get up and he'd only laugh at me after he knew I was safe. I need someone who will always be himself, by my side, someone who would make me feel at home again. I officially "moved out" from Adam, metaphorically, of course.

I got home and fell into my soft, warm bed. Snowflake jumped up next to me and put his two front paws on me. Snowflake always felt my pain and he could ease it with his signs of affection. Strangely enough, I wasn't in pain anymore. I just wanted to sleep and finish my article.

The next day, on my sixth try, I set out to finish my article. There were so many more arguments against online dating. Reading each account, it always seemed to be a matter of luck in terms of who you got. You could write whatever you wanted about yourself and it was possible that daydreaming in front of your computer you may feel that you'd finally found someone you seemed to click with, of course only in the beginning. But then you went on a date. The guy turned out to be completely different, you couldn't even squeeze out one full sentence. If we really think about it, we have the same chance of finding someone decent online as in a bar. The only difference is that if you meet a guy in a bar and he's 6 ft in the beginning, he won't shrink in the restroom, all night he stays 6 ft even at your next meeting. But if someone writes on their profile that they're 6 ft it can easily happen that on your date a 5.2 "tall" little liar walks up to you. I signed in with my fake profile and I checked how many ravenous fish wanted to take a bite of my Melissa. Wow, forty-five new messages! There were thirty I didn't even open because the beginning was already so terrible, I knew I couldn't survive reading to the end. Some messages where so embarrassingly bizarre, I just stared at the screen.

"Hey, beautiful. You're the only cactus in this desert!"

I'd have been curious to know what he expected as a good reply, "Come and water me, oh knight in shining armour?"

There were a couple nice ones waiting for me also.

"Yo, girl! Your face is pretty and the rest of the package too? See you sometime?"

I could already hear the 50 cent song as a soundtrack in my head "Yo, yo, yo, lil' mamma!"

After I read all of that, I had a good laugh and finally finished my article, I wondered what I could do to skip the school party next week, even though it was organised by Violet. There will be people from outside the school, so at least the haunting presence of Cassie and Adam would melt into the crowd. Plus I'd already promised Violet that I'd go, so I couldn't let her down.

I promised myself that I'd share everything important with Ruby, so although I wanted to forget about the whole thing, I didn't want to keep secrets from her. I told her about my date with Aaron, the kiss, Adam's kiss and I asked her to not to say anything to anyone about it. She promised me that she would snip off Adam's balls during the night. She also told me that Adam was quite upset when he got home on Saturday night and Cassie wasn't with him. She suspected they'd had a fight, but when she asked Adam, he told her to drop it and that he'd move out as soon as his book was finished. Good, he should get out of there, that's what I told Ruby, but I felt my heart sink. I could hardly breathe. Yes, he should leave, that would be the best for everyone, I didn't want to see him again in this life, or the next one.

Ruby asked me about Aaron. She began to annoy me because she asked a million times if I was sure that I didn't care about him, if I wasn't sad? Wasn't it quite obvious that all I cared about was getting over the king of jerks?

Now that my love life was reduced to zero, I handed in all my homework on time and I had no one to daydream about, since I'd exiled Adam from my pink clouds, I had a lot of time to read. I avoided depressive or overly cheesy stories and I tried to enrich my soul with entertaining and upbeat stories.

I liked one book a lot. The protagonist has a crush on this guy, yeah I know, there's a gazillion books that start out like this. The boy doesn't care about the girl, well this could be us, although the girl does everything for the boy to notice her.

The girl suddenly disappears and the boy begins to wonder where she is and he starts to miss her, but she's no more. I tried to avoid so much cheesy bullshit, but that's how far I'd got.

We were different though because it was Adam who was going to disappear after he'd finished his stupid book. I didn't need his absence to figure it all out, I already knew that I loved him.

So, let's get the party started. Maybe I'll get to know another jerk who could keep me from thinking of Adam. I wouldn't even mind if he was a bigger asshole than the previous ones, as long as he helps distract my mind from Adam.


Beware what you wish for


Most girls have *The Dress*. The dress is more or less the piece you buy for special occasions, completely disregarding the price, so that whenever that random special occasion comes, you wear The Dress. Sadly, these dresses tend to wait forever in the bottom of our wardrobe for that big day when we can finally wear it. However, this day never comes. We buy newer and newer special dresses until we find our wardrobe full with dresses we bought for important occasions but which we never wore.

After long hesitations I chose a dress covered in bluish-green feathers, convinced that this dress had been made for me and that nothing could keep me from going to the party in it. This nice feeling lasted until the moment I arrived in our living room. I saw dad poking mum and whispering to her. Of course, loud enough for me to hear it.

"Hey, I didn't notice it was already Halloween!"

"What are you saying, Robert! Our daughter is beautiful like always."

Yeah, a mother always finds her daughter the most beautiful, while dads are always hilariously honest.

"I wasn't denying her beauty, I was just wondering how many poor birds were skinned for her dress."

Dad had always been critical about these kinds of things. I don't think I've ever had a dress he hasn't commented on. I dragged myself back upstairs, somewhat hurt and dived into my wardrobe again. I couldn't go to the party wearing a whole zoo after all. I slipped out from my feathery "costume" and looked for something else. *It should be simple… ah this one should do the trick.* I pulled out an old asymmetric piece which shone in different shades of turquoise. I'd completely forgotten about it. The last time I wore it was… well, let's just forget about it. Okay, last time

I wore it was when Dylan broke up with me. I should have hated this dress because of the bad memories, but today I think back to that day with a sense of relief that I got rid of that jackass. So now, I was free to love this dress, especially because it was a nice example that even the most stubborn heartbreak passes. When I threw this dress at the bottom of my wardrobe, I thought my life was over and I'd become a dusty skeleton. Now I had a good many Dylans behind my back and I could proudly say that it's never the end of the world. Okay, now I have Adam instead of Dylan, but with time someone new will come.

They should come. There was someone new then and there will be someone new now.

To hell with Dylan! This dress was beautiful. I slipped into it and hurried down because Ruby had been waiting for me in front of our house. On the way out, I caught dad's newest remark.

"First, she was a peacock, now she's a mermaid! I'm telling you, it's Halloween!"

I ignored dad's sarcastic comments and bid them good bye with a "Bye, I'll be back!" and I ran out to Ruby's. It took me two very fast steps to cover the way from our door to Ruby's car parking on the front lawn. She wore the usual little black dress and told me that Violet was going to have some of her friends at the party and she'd want to introduce us. *Great, who the hell wants to meet new people?* I managed to resist asking Ruby if Adam was coming tonight. Knowing Cassie, she was surely going to be there, but Adam didn't really seem like a party animal.

When we got to the school, I realized that I'd forgotten someone: Aaron. We hadn't met since that certain exchange of texts because I managed to avoid him during the week, but I knew it wouldn't be possible now. Especially since he was standing in front of the school with half of the football team. Yay, one of those awkward moments. I couldn't even pretend to not see him because our eyes locked already when I got out of the car. We politely greeted each other, although I imagined deep down he wished to see me burning on a stake. We walked passed them and entered the school. Violet had called me at least ten times, but I only managed to hear it this time.

"Where the hell are you?"

"We're already here, don't worry, we just popped into the restrooms to perfect our looks."

I could hear that Violet was super excited, although I didn't really get why, when she'd already organized tons of other parties. *It must be some new guy.* Ruby was also dolled up, as if she had someone new on her radar, which was quite interesting since I didn't know about it and we'd agreed that there were no more secrets. Yep, no secrets. I'd already ran into Aaron, so there was only one more embarrassing thing left.

We looked around to see what Violet had done with the place: we could barely recognise the school. Violet had a real gift for these kinds of things, she had turned the school into a real club. Nobody would think of the embarrassing interrogations or Sport classes struggling with handstands, the only thing which came to mind was that it felt great to be here. The boring old school turned into a beach hotel with hundreds of young people who wanted to party. Hundreds minus one, me, who had absolutely no wish to be here, but everybody else was pretty thrilled.

We found Violet at the bar erected in the great hall. As we entered, I spotted her in the ring of three boys. I guess one of them was the reason for all the excitement. We walked up to them and introduced ourselves. I figured our right away which was the one Violet was so excited about. His name was Oliver, he had dark hair and brown eyes. I had no idea about the length of his hair because he was wearing a black beanie. I could only congratulate him on his fashion choice, it made a lot of sense to arrive at a hot party area with a beanie on our head. A real hipster. He reminds me of people who wear sunglasses in the middle of the night. Anyway, I knew what he was playing at: he looked very good in that beanie and the matching plain shirt.

I don't remember the name of the other two guys, because they only mumbled it to themselves and I didn't have the time to riddle it out. One might start with a P, the other with a T. The two nameless heroes went to get drinks, while Oliver stayed with us. Great! I wanted to catch up with Violet, but I held back with Oliver there. Ruby told me that she was going to have a look but would be back soon. *Thanks a lot, abandon me to be the third wheel.* I wanted to leave, but I remembered Cassie and Adam. How lame it would be if they arrived and found me standing at the bar all alone. No way! I'll stay to be the unwanted third wheel. Violet and Oliver barely talked. I tried to engage them in conversation, but all they gave me was a "yeah" or an "okay." Oliver told us that he would look for the others, but would be back later. *You don't have to hurry back!* Of course, when he looked at me, I nodded, smiling. Then I gave Violet an ugly look.

"So, who's he?"

"Oliver? He's not important, he's just a friend of Timber's.

"Timber, like the song? And who's cute? One of the silent ones or the boy who wouldn't take his beanie off for the world?

"You're weird, Amy. Timber is just his nickname, the real one is Thomas and I'm completely smitten with him."

Did I hear the word "smitten" correctly?

"What do you mean by smitten? How long have you known him?"

Although I have no right to judge her because I can grow lifelong feelings for a complete stranger in a matter of mere seconds.

"Violet, I think you haven't been filling me in on certain things lately."

"We're having another date with Thomas tomorrow. I've known him for a while now, but we had the break through moment during the last party. You must know what I mean?"

Of course, I knew. I fell apart inside as memories of walking with Adam flashed in front of my eyes, or when I'd still believed in us and I went to see him to confess all my feelings. You know the feeling when somebody's mere presence makes you happy even though you're not a couple yet. Why can't this be now? Why is the feeling that inspired me before now killing me?

Thomas 'the steam engine' came back to entertain Violet and I made myself scarce. Where could Ruby be? I went on a prowl and I found myself in the company of Oliver who was also looking for his friends. We couldn't find either Ruby or Oliver's other nameless friend. Oliver suddenly looked at me and said, laughing:

"Hey, mademoiselle, fancy pulling shapes with me? I'm an awful dancer, but maybe we could encourage the rest of the nitwits who're huddling in the corners."

His question was as random as our getting to know each other. The music was nice and even though I wasn't a star dancer either, I didn't mind "pulling shapes" with him. The dance floor was almost empty, and I felt like I hadn't drunk enough for this. He held out his hand and I gave him mine. An old hit blared from the loudspeakers and Oliver, well… he didn't lie about his inaptitude when it came to dancing. It was sort of charming though, the way he was moving his thin little legs. We made up our own choreography and soon enough we found ourselves surrounded by equally clumsy teenagers. The party started and I needed to drink something, I dragged Oliver along. Finally, I was having a good time. That night, Oliver was my consolation for all the suffering of the previous weeks. I poured my heart out to him, poor thing must have been bored to death. Especially because I bet, he'd never heard the word "Adam" so many times in under one hour. He also opened up to me, telling me all about the girls he liked in his school, but who always ignored him. I had never heard a boy open up to me like that, so his words touched my heart. He reminded me of Aaron. I didn't realise how much I might have hurt him. I was about to plunge into self-reproach when something happened. My eyes were attracted to the far end of the room. The air froze in the whole room, or maybe just around me. He stood in the entrance. He, who was able to destroy everything, myself included, with his mere presence. He wore a blue shirt and blue jeans, not really a party outfit. I didn't see Cassie by his side, so he probably arrived alone.

*I have to go to restroom, right now!* I told Oliver I'd be back soon although I actually had no idea what I was about to do. My legs turned into jelly. I hated it. I walked forward on trembling legs, past the students lined up along the wall, I felt incredibly lame. I didn't go to the toilet, but to look for Adam. I gave up fighting myself, I wanted to see him. I wanted to feel his smell, the warmth of his jumper, another one because I still had the one from last time. I felt as if I was running a race against time, like in a game. Can you find what we hid in two minutes? My eyes had already scanned all the faces of the school, but I couldn't see him. I felt the disappointment. He had to see me, and I had to see him. I was wearing my prettiest dress. He had to see me in it and then the miracle would happen and he would realise that he was also in love with me. Of course, it was completely impossible without the dress. But this outfit had magical powers.

I was walking past the Biology classroom when someone grabbed my arm and pulled me into the room. This was the most remote part of the school. It was him. He was my kidnapper! He was clutching my hand so hard that he almost broke it, but I didn't mind. My love is strong like Hulk! He is a superhero after all. He pushed a lock of my hair behind my ear with one hand, while the other still held me. He eased the pressure, so I stopped worrying that he might break my hand, he just held me softly. Just like at the beginning of a date when a boy holds a girl's hand for the first time.

He took a coin from his pocket and asked me:

"Heads or tails?"

What's his deal with his stupid coin?

"Tails," I answered in a confident voice, but my face mirrored my confusion.

Instead of sweeping me off my feet, he's playing coin games with me?

He threw the coin up and slammed it on his hand. My heart beat frantically and I felt that if something didn't happen to calm it down, it would jump out of my chest. It was heads. He put the coin back to his pocket and let go of my hand. I thought it was the end and he would walk away. I stared at him in confusion and I caught us staring at each other's lips. Okay, he had two minutes left to kiss me. What was he waiting for? It was clear as day that I'd given him a sign and I wasn't going to punch him this time, so he should just make a move. He leant to my ear and whispered that I'd lost. I'd already given up my every hope about him when he spoke again.

If it hadn't been tails, I would have kissed you. If it was heads...

He ran his fingers across my hair and pushed me against the wall. He kissed the corner of my mouth slowly then looked into my eyes again.

"Well, if it had been heads, I'd done the same."

He softly laid his hand on the back of my neck and pulled me closer. He kissed me on the lips in a way that every cell in my body caught fire. That's the feeling I associated with kisses in films. This was the kiss which would make your foot kind of pop. My foot managed to pop just enough to kick the skeleton, who we affectionately christened Joey. Both of Joey's arms fell to the ground from the impact of my foot. This was really an unforgettable kiss on every level. Whenever I'll think of that kiss it takes me to my happy place and makes me laugh. We tried marvelling at each other but we couldn't keep it up for even a minute before we burst out laughing.

I was in love with him. I felt that our story was fulfilled in that moment. His kiss was longer than the ones before and his touch melted my whole body more intensely than I'd imagined. I didn't want the moment to end, I didn't want him to walk away again. I didn't want to live my life without him being a part of it. I loved him and we both needed to deal with it.

I didn't want to go back to find the others. I wanted to stay with Adam all evening long. I understood, with sadness in my heart that our moment was over. He took my hand and led me out of the room. I was full of questions, but didn't dare ask any of them. I knew my questions would just ruin the mood. I felt how the evening would end, but I didn't feel nervous. I waited for the moment to finally be with him. When we were leaving, I tried to drag him towards the exit because I didn't want to meet Oliver after having spent an hour bitching about Adam, while now I was sauntering with him, hand in hand, as if nothing had happened.

Passing through the great hall we spotted Aaron having a fight with a boy from outside the school. Two lanterns had already lost their life in the fight; they lay on the ground broken into pieces. I spotted the worrying face of Ruby in the crowd and I ran to her. She told me everything while Adam tried to separate the boys engaged in a seemingly fight to the death. Apparently one of the slightly drunk boys bothered Ruby and Aaron came to her rescue. In the end Adam and another boy managed to separate the two fighters. The crowd lost interest and soon everybody went back into the party to dance.

Ruby stayed with Aaron and I started looking for Adam, but he was gone. Seconds before he was by my side and now, I couldn't find him anywhere. He couldn't have just left me there. We couldn't be running the same endless circles again!

I had to find him immediately!

I ran into the gymnasium because I couldn't find him anywhere in the corridors. My eyes scanned every possible nook and cranny, although I was sure he wasn't hiding in any of the corners. I didn't care about anything else, but finding him. Oliver was at the same place I left him, but was now talking with a different girl. I was heading back to Ruby when Oliver spotted me. He jumped up and walked towards me. He tried to figure out why I disappeared, but I was simply unable to explain. We stared at each other somewhat dumbly, when he asked me if I was OK. I told him that I was, and I was about to say goodbye to him when he took my hand and turned me to face him.

"Can I take you home? You just give me the sign and we're out of here."

If Adam hadn't been here, I'd have probably melted, but he was there. I didn't exactly know where, but the main thing was that I was with him.

"Oliver, the thing is…"

I didn't manage to finish my sentence, because Adam appeared out of thin air.

"Ah, here you are! I've been looking for you everywhere!"

Where, under the ground?

I gave Oliver a fleeting glance, but he got the situation. He didn't comment or anything, just leaned closer to me and whispered loudly enough for Adam to hear it too:

"Amy, if there's anything wrong, you call me. Okay?"

"Sure, but I'll be okay."

How could I call him? I didn't even know his number and I knew I was safe with Adam by my side. Anyway, I've only known Oliver for a few hours. Adam didn't really get what was going on and he gave suspicious looks to Oliver. Outside we met Ruby and Aaron who seemed to be getting along pretty well. Adam joked about the fact that luckily, he was a family member and surely wouldn't end up with Ruby after me. He didn't know that I wouldn't let him go anyway because he was meant for me. On the way home, I thought about Oliver's words. Why treat Adam like a bad guy? Okay, I'd cried because of him, but I overreacted, he wasn't really a bad guy, actually he was the best. I loved him and that was the end of the story.

The rain was pouring outside, I wouldn't have cared even if we had to walk home. Adam changed everything: the road, the landscape, my thoughts and me too. We arrived at their house, but he asked me not to get out of the car just yet. *No way, I hope he doesn't want to take me home. I gave myself up to him,*

*I'm his through and through he should just take me, for heaven's sake!*

He got out of the car and walked over to my side. He opened the door, took off his jumper and put it over my head.

"Run inside, I'll be right behind you."

Another jumper, another moment from a romantic movie, another feeling that could have killed me. I wanted to follow his orders, but I couldn't. I looked at him and kissed him. I didn't care about the rain or anything else that could have changed the ending of our story. I wouldn't have cared about tornadoes, hailstorms or volcanoes. I hugged him and he put his arms around my waist.

"Why don't we continue this inside?" he asked with a freezing voice.

Adam probably didn't look at the kissing in the rain thing like I did. For me, it was romantic, for him it was "Why are we soaking outside when we could be inside?" Men! I went in the house, he parked the car and followed me. Ruby's parents were sleeping, so we sneaked upstairs to the guestroom which was temporarily Adam's dominion.

The evening was wonderful, nothing like the first one we spent together. Although my memories of that night were a bit hazy, but I knew that this one was completely different. I'd like to add that he was sober and so was I. Everything had changed: his kiss, his touch, everything. I'd never felt this way before. Everything happened as it should. I was the happiest girl in the whole wild word. He embraced me, I cuddled even closer against him. We talked until dawn. I don't remember when we fell asleep, but I remember getting a goodnight kiss. In the morning when I woke up, I was so happy I forgot to sneak around. We were finally together, or something like that and the ice was finally broken. I glanced next to myself, but the bed was empty. More precisely, Adam's side was empty. I went down to the kitchen to ask Ruby where Adam was. He must have sneaked out to the shop for our favourite cornflakes or for some cheap copy because it wasn't available here. I found Ruby alone in the kitchen. When I got downstairs I immediately started telling her everything when Ruby stopped me.

"Amy!"

"No, Ruby, you don't need to say anything. I've never been this happy. I'm in love with him and it's not some kind of fake love, so many people make up for themselves. It's real. He is the exception on my "he's really different list.""

"Amy…"

Ruby was paler than white.

"What's wrong? I'm sorry, you should tell me about your evening! What's up with Aaron?"

"Amy, it's about Adam. He's gone."

"When will he be back?"

Ruby froze and I started to feel strange myself.

"He's not coming back, he's gone for good."

I ran back to the room and looked around. The room was as empty as I felt inside. There was only one thing in the room: a book on the dusty desk. On the cover a boy stood next to a girl making faces. Written by Adam Baker.

Preface: At the end of a story people always expect some big twist. They breeze through the whole story, full of excitement, while they're trying to guess the end. The end that would bring fulfilment, that would make up for all the trials the protagonists had to go through. However, not every story has a happy ending and sometimes one doesn't even understand what the point of the whole thing was. Sometimes when something ends, the story still continues because it's still not the big endgame. There are stories which never end. Amy, maybe our story is like this.

# Chapter Seven

Three, two, one, HAPPY NEW YEAR!

A million kisses must have been given in that moment, tons of resolutions made and uncountable texts lost in the void because of the over-saturated networks. At the same time, many people could close a period and open a new one. It'd been the new year for exactly a minute when he came up to me and kissed me on the lips. I'd been scanning the crowd for him for around fifteen minutes and I was about to give up my new year's kiss when he appeared in front of me.

"You're one minute late." I chided him, but gave him the "it's so great that you're here" look.

"Yeah, for a moment I contemplated who I should kiss, but I looked around and you were the only one free," said this twenty-first century Romeo. A dumb smile appeared on his face and I wanted to pay back his kind comment by punching him hard in his shoulder, but he caught my arm and pulled me closer.

"Amy, I couldn't be late for us, even if I wanted to. We'll always be on time."

He leaned closer to me to whisper something in my ear:

"I love you."

The three words thousands of women would kill to hear and thousands would break up over, if they're not pronounced at that exact time and in the way they imagined it. I never felt the weight or the real meaning of this simple sentence, but finally I also dared to say it:

"I love you too, Oliver!"

Three months ago I couldn't even imagine that I'd have somebody in my life. I must've looked exactly as bad as the girl in that lame movie, who stares out of the window, watching the seasons change while crying after her lost love who had a face like a box. The only difference for me was that I wasn't mourning a vampire with super-abilities, but a mere human. Luckily, this allowed me to cram one year of suffering into a mere three months. Okay, I have to tell you that the maximum amount of time I could spend sitting in that suffering position was half an hour, but the rest was pretty accurate.

I watched the yellow leaves falling from the tree and I wished a huge meteor would fall on the current location of Adam with the same slow determination. It didn't mean that I hated him. He didn't do anything wrong, just tricked me, humiliated me, betrayed me, made me fall for him, drove me mad, annihilated me, why should I hate him? I really don't.

I knew very well what I should feel. I should have hated him. Hated him for what he did to me, but I couldn't think of him that way. Autumn went by in this mindset: I hated all the men in the world, my life, the whole wild world and myself. I went through all the phases. In the first phase, I cried like a baby and thought my life was over. In the second phase, I felt fine one minute, even started to see the light at the end of the tunnel, the next minute someone blocked the light: Adam. This lasted for a while, then I passed to the last phase. I felt a little bit better, emphasis on the "little bit" and I felt that I was finally over him. I met someone, so I figured it was finally over. I believed that it had really all passed and that I was finally ready for a new relationship. But then I stood broken after the first kiss and I didn't understand why I couldn't forget. I gave up on the hope that I'd ever get over him, when the magic happened. I didn't want to delete him from existence or from my heart. I let him go.

You may believe that it'll never pass, but suddenly you catch yourself no longer looking for his motions in everyone, eventually if someone with similar looks walks past you on the street, you just walk on by. You don't miss him anymore. You learn to live with his absence. When will you be over it? Maybe in a month. Maybe in a few years. It's also possible that you may never get over him, it. Time washes away your pain and although it won't disappear completely, it will make it fade away, as the sea washes away the sand. Your heart will have peace again. I left time for everything, and when I least expected it, a new someone walked into my life.

He turned my head just as Adam did. The whole story started about one month after Mr. Jerk disappeared. After he walked out of the door without saying as much as a word, only leaving me his shitty book, I felt that it was high time that I drove him out of my life, once and for all. In that piece of turd he called a book, that he left me to make in an attempt to make it impossible for me to forget him, he left me a note: "Please read me!"

*Of course, I'm going to take a chance and read your book, just like you gave a chance for you and me.* I took the book and threw it in the first trash I found. *Coward,* I thought to myself. At least you could have mustered the courage to tell me in person that you didn't want me. No, he had to run away.

In the first few days, I avoided the others, including Ruby. Oliver tried to reach me a couple of times, but I never answered. I thought he pitied me like the others. I was too busy wallowing in my sorrow, I didn't need anybody's pity, it'd have made me even more miserable. He's gone, so what? That's how much the whole thing meant for him, why should I care more than he does? That's what I told myself in the vain attempt to soothe my mind. It worked for a little while, then I was back on the suffering train. One day when I was walking out of the school, I saw Oliver standing next to the building. *You can't turn away, Amy, it's too late, he's noticed you.*

I pretended to be nonchalant, and knowing that I couldn't have avoided him, I smiled at him and gave him a confident "Hello!" Anybody who knows me, would have noticed that this "hello" was as confident as my answer to the question *Are you really over Adam?*

"Amy, did my eyes deceive me when I saw that you wanted to turn and avoid meeting me?"

"No way, I'm really happy to see you! I've just forgotten something at school, but I'll get it tomorrow, it's not that urgent."

Make a convincing face!

"Sure, you forgot something. Maybe the location of the emergency exit?"

Ah, my convincing face has failed me.

He chuckled, then changed the topic to a more serious subject, frowning. He asked why I didn't answer any of his messages.

I couldn't really tell him that I was in the heyday of my "I don't give a sh*t" period and that Adam destroyed me and I was sitting around on the ruins of my life."

Oliver looked completely different than during our first meeting. He didn't have his signature beanie and I was happy to see that he had quite nice hair. His plan was to take me home and assist me in fuming about Adam.

It seemed like a great idea and Oliver was a perfect accomplice.

He was funny. I liked that. He also told me that I'd deserved what I got because I was silly and blind. He didn't feel sorry for me like the others and it helped. He said what he really thought, and he didn't try to reassure me with pointless illusions that Adam would come back, or that he would realise what he had lost and B.S. like that. These things are only good to soothe the pain for a little while. Oliver didn't beat around the bush, he said what Ruby and my other friends didn't dare say, and he said the things that I had problems admitting to myself: Adam wasn't coming back, or at least not for me. Even if he came back, nothing would happen. He'd left me once, what would I actually need with him? I needed Oliver and his brutal honestly.

He managed to conquer the woman of his dreams and it reassured me. First because it proved that there were exceptions, secondly because this way I didn't need to worry if this thing between us could morph into something more than friendship. We spent too much time together. I thought too much about him when we weren't together and this disturbed me. I didn't understand myself: I wasn't over Adam, he still lived in my heart, but its other half slowly got requisitioned by

Oliver.

It might have begun after the party Violet organized for me. The official theme was "Y.O.L.O.", but I knew it could have been "Let's Bring Amy Back To Reality."

The only reason I went was because of Oliver. It drove me insane when I was with him and also when I wasn't. Maybe if that night next to the bonfire he hadn't given me that look, if I hadn't leaned my head on his shoulder out of habit, if I hadn't stumbled three times in front of him on purpose, nudging him to help me up, the whole thing would never have happened. I might have been hiding behind the "maybe" and I never admiting, not even to myself, that we had something going on for quite a while. I guess it might have actually started on that day when he hugged me. It was different than before. Something changed in the way he looked at me and I knew the same thing happened to me as well. Until that moment he was my Oliver, my friend, the guy who had a girlfriend.

I went for a walk to rethink everything: Adam, Oliver, what was happening to me. He came after me. He didn't run away. Oliver was supposed to come with his girlfriend, but he arrived alone. He told me that they'd had a fight about *something* and he decided to come alone. By the end of the evening I'd learnt that *that something* was me. We spent too much time together and it bothered his girlfriend. For a while I argued with Oliver and told him that maybe we shouldn't see each other for a while, although I would have found it impossible, Oliver too. That's when the maybes started, that's when the looks changed. There was no kiss, just a hug and walking hand in hand. I hated myself. I was Cassie in this story. The girl who stole someone else. Okay, let's go on!

I was so immersed in riddling out my relationship with Oliver, that I didn't realise what was going on around me. One day Ruby grabbed me in the school corridor and called me aside. I couldn't say if I disappeared from her life or she from mine. I missed her, but she always reminded me of Adam.

"Amy, we have to talk!"

My brain tried to come up with a good speech to explain the reasons for my disappearance when she continued:

"I can't keep it a secret anymore. Amy I love you a lot and you're my best friend."

"Come on, Ruby, get it out!"

It was somewhat scary listening to her bossing herself around and also thinking about what she could have done.

"I forgive you in advance just spill it already!"

"Alright. I'm in love with Aaron."

The Aaron she wanted to hook me up with? The one we called Calvin Aaron Klein behind his back? No way! Okay, I knew love couldn't be controlled, but I sometimes felt like flipping love off, hoping that Amor's arrow was just kidding.

It disturbed me. Aaron was my last home. I imagined the rest of my life in the following way: if I didn't find the crazy, all-burning love until I'm sixty, or if I found it, but it remained unrequited, then I'd still have Aaron as a last resort. I know it sounds pretty bitchy, but it's not any worse than what Adam did to me. Life vs. me: 1 – 1.

In this new setup, I saw my lonely skeleton falling apart on a remote bench. On one hand, I had no idea what I should say, on the other hand I really started to worry that Ruby and I fell so much apart. This stupid feeling again.

Our friendship couldn't go this way, we weren't like this. I felt the whole thing so confusing that I wanted to run away. This is also his fault. If I had the chance, I'd go after him and slap him. If everything hadn't reminded me of him, then maybe I wouldn't have avoided my friends and I wouldn't have ended up having a half-crush on Oliver.

I blamed Adam for everything although deep inside I knew that I was the only one to blame for my messed up relationships. I grew apart from Ruby which was unacceptable. I'll fix it; I had to fix it. I was unable to feel angry with her. I was the one to send Aaron away because I fell in love with a full-time asshole. I might've really deserved what I got, but I had no reason to be mad at Ruby. Especially since I never cared about Aaron, he was just the last resort to avoid being buried alone.

I wanted to get back to the point from where I wandered away.

"I want to hear every tiny detail from the first "I want more" feeling, to the first kiss and everything."

I saw signs of relief appearing on her face and a few teardrops rolled out from the corner or her eyes, but they disappeared so quickly that I had no time to draw attention to them. From the open-armed, tear-shedding hug, I felt that she also forgave me.

"I don't even know which question to ask you first: if you're mad at me because of Aaron or if you're aware how much I missed you? You can never disappear again, did you get it?"

She grabbed my shoulders and started shaking me, repeating "never" at least ten times.

"I p-r-o-m-i-s-e," I said.

She finally stopped after she'd shaken agreement out from me and I was impatient to hear about her story with Aaron.

"No! I'm not telling you anything until you understand that I need you. You're my bestest friend and I'm not going to tolerate you ignoring me because of such a lame loser. I hope I've been clear."

I understood what she said, and I agreed with every word of it, especially the part about Adam being a lame loser. I couldn't have said it better, myself.

I've been wrong, I've made a mistake, I know. But he was different, really. I think so even now and that's why it hurts so much. With the others this feeling evaporated quickly, but not with him. I wanted it to go away so much, I wanted to think of him the same way I think of all the others, but I couldn't. To this very day, I feel like it would have been a mistake. It was true, painful, but real. I was in love with him and somewhere deep down, part of me still might be. But I let him go because however awful it might sound, he's not for me. *Well, according to him. According to me, we're a match made in heaven.*

He'll make someone happy, but that someone is not me. I really don't mind, at all. And you know why? Because I've never felt this way. I've never been so much in love with someone and if the price is that it has to hurt, so be it. I've got to realise that I messed up a lot of things because of things. I'd like you to take me back into your circle of best friends. I want to renew our best friend promise we made when we were small. I'd like to cry your pillow full of tears while watching Brazilian soap operas and envying the perfect looks of those women. I'd like to slide among the trees on our sledge decorated with reindeer, while you can barely breathe from laughing so hard. I want to have these meaningless little things back in my life, so that we can fill them with meaning. I want to laugh with you about nothing, sometimes for hours. I want our shared things to last and I want new ones. I want everything to be back as it was.

Ruby tensed all her facial muscles to avoid bursting with laughter. She cleared her throat to finish the conversation about the future of our friendship with a quote from our favourite childhood book.

"We'll move past this as well because that's how real friendship works. We move on even if we've messed up, even if we don't know which way to go. In the end we always wait for the other if she got stuck half way, we'll start again. Yes, again from the very beginning."

I could only agree with Jenny Watson's touching quote and Ruby's forgiving look.

"I don't know where to begin. You know there was that night, although maybe I should skip it because of my jerk of a half-brother, but that's when everything started. After the fight Aaron was sitting alone on the stairs in front of the school and I went up to him to say thanks for having protected me. He answered, very chivalrously, that it was nothing and I gave him a hug. We started talking and the next time I looked it was half past two. You know Aaron, he's a gentleman, so he insisted on taking me home. I refused, but when he offered it a second time, I gave in. Nothing happened, but lying in bed at night, I kept seeing him as he leaves the football field, sweaty and with his red face and he walks towards me to finally kiss me. Yes, I'm ashamed to say that I became just like the girls we used to laugh about. I became one of his fans although I'd never have imagined it could happen to me. I always tried to "accidentally" run into him, so that he would notice the coincidences. Of course, without him noticing that it was me orchestrating each coincidences. To cut a long story short, I was lying wait, hoping that he'd notice me at one point. Me, the girl who never cared about younger boys managed to open Pandora's box again."

"Aaron is older than us."

"You know me. I don't care as long as the age difference is not more than ten years."

"I didn't dare tell you because a.) nothing happened, b.) I knew Aaron had been in love with you since the beginning of times. Also."

Her voice went all squealy and she also fiddled with her fingers.

"There was a party the week before New Year's Eve. You had been gone for a while. And you know how violent Violet can get when it comes to parties, and I also knew that Aaron would be there, so as a number one fangirl, I also had to be there. The party was horrible. It was full of girls from school that I hate, for example Cassie. She was visibly over Adam because she appeared hand in hand with Dennis, her male counterpart when it comes to evilness. I wondered how they found each other only now, since they could do much more evil together than alone. I set out to find Violet to say goodbye and to leave that terrible party behind. Of course, I managed to run into Aaron in the gate, just like in some lame rom com. He begged me to stay, but didn't manage to convince me. I sort of half got over the idea that he and I could ever. So I bid him goodnight. I left Becca's house, but I only got to the bus stop because someone called after me:

"Can I drive you home?"

Drumroll.

Who could it be? Let's pull the curtain! Yes, it was him. The big question. The crowd is going wild, and I... Of course, he could drive me home. I didn't feel like walking home through god knows how many kilometres with something

89

drizzling from the sky and you know how much I hate it when my hair loses its perfect shape. The version I gave Aaron was a nonchalant, "Yeah sure, if you're going in my direction." I elegantly disregarded the fact that he lived in the opposite side of town." It was the typical "deep inside you've already given up on him, but then he comes back and rewrites everything" situation with Aaron and Ruby in the lead roles.

"On the way, he asked if I felt like stopping to have a hot chocolate or something. *Stopping somewhere, being with him, having a hot chocolate? Yes, yes and yes!* I gave a big yes to everything that had anything to do with Aaron. I was in love with him. Of course, it was a bit difficult not to think of him as the boy who had a crush on you for so many years. Maybe that's why I found it difficult in the beginning to take him and our "hot chocolate night" seriously. I got to know his side, he was literally hiding under his "Aaron Klein" model looks. I felt exactly like after the school party. I had a crush on him again.

It wasn't like those awkward dates where you feign interest and if the other drinks his coffee with two sugars that's what you do as well, in order to show how much you have in common. No, with Aaron I could really be myself. We both hated coffee and not because the other did too, but because we were disgusted by its smell. He hated horror movies, I loved them. He loved Science, I wanted to love it, if only I could understand what it was about. He was excellent in Spanish and I was great in French, I don't know what this one means, but the point is that we complement each other! He likes to sleep on the left side of the bed, while I like to sleep on the right. His favourite colour is black, mine is white. We belong together like yin and yang. Do you understand? I love chocolate, he's a health fanatic. So if I buy a bar of chocolate I won't need to be worried that he'll eat it. If, on the other hand, he buys a vegetable plate, he won't need to stress that I'll steal his carrots like a little rabbit. He's my exact opposite, but I think that's why something started that night. I could finally be myself and him too. Did you know that when he was a child, Aaron was bitten by a dog and he's been terrified of them ever since? Of course, whenever he's in company he just says he's not fond of dogs because he doesn't want to admit that in his boyhood he was attacked by a beastly Yorkshire terrier. Yes, a tiny dog, but the memory still haunts Aaron. So this is how our story started. I don't expect you to understand it because I know that many things could sound silly, but still."

Ruby's childlike enthusiasm made me forget everything.

I suddenly felt like in the beginning of my story when I tried to repress my feelings for Adam, but eventually had to accept that it was impossible.

I finally started to get back on my feet, thanks to Oliver. I can't put a label on our relationship, and I have no idea how we were doing. Oliver's the exact opposite of Adam and we shouldn't forget the most important bit of information: Oliver still hasn't abandoned me, although he had millions of occasions to. I could count on him so I didn't need to worry about waking up alone one day. We're more than friends, but I don't know if it's love. If I look at the fact that I couldn't spend a day without him, then I guess it was.

I was looking forward to the weekend because Oliver wanted to talk to me. I thought he might want to tell me he loved me and I could finally give up my role as an unattainable girl.

After the trauma Adam caused me, I promised myself that I'd never be in love again. Alright, I managed to break my promise pretty quickly, so I made a new one. I'm never going to display my emotions. Alright, I was starting to break this one as well, shit! Finally, Oliver makes up not the whole ninety-nine percent of my thoughts, but only eighty percent so I had to take the opportunity to give a chance to someone else. And Oliver did really interest me.

Come on, Oliver, what are you waiting for! He's late. He has five minutes to walk in through that door. Four, three…

My Oliver countdown clock was on two when he finally arrived. I was excited although I didn't really know why. I knew that this was going to be the part when we try to untangle our emotions. He was going to confess his feelings to me and I'd bat my eyelashes and tell him I felt the same. It all seemed so easy.

In the beginning, everything always seems so easy. There's the guy you like. You've been eyeing each other for a while and maybe there's something going on between the two of you. You believe that something special has happened and you believe that it's going to be different with him. Maybe it will. Then the perfect boy becomes the perfect disappointment because you've misinterpreted the signs, because maybe 'the signs' were only visible to you. Who knows? Maybe it actually will work out and he really is the one meant only for you, but never forget that life isn't easy. It cannot be.

If I tell you that life can be full of surprises, you'll laugh at me. If I tell you that you won't get anywhere close to the place you're currently seeking, you'll just wave your hand at me, saying *Sure thing*. If I tell you that you'll remember this one sentence, you'll seemingly agree but in a few years you'll think back and remember this sentence no matter where you might be.

I wanted to go for a walk with Oliver although it was the middle of January, or to put it in Ruby's words, it was "the season of fat snowmen." It only meant that I had to wear three jumpers in order not to freeze to death and then I had to squeeze myself into my puff-coat, in the end, I looked like a fat snowman myself and could barely move thanks to all my layers.

Yeah, this wasn't the best period to conquer hearts with our looks, a snowman moving like the terminator would catch nobody's eyes.

It was a struggle, but in the end I managed to pull my coat over my two jumpers. I had to try it twice, but eventually I managed to fit into my snowman-outfit with a few twists and turns. Oliver was waiting in front of our house in the cold, until mum invited him in for hot tea. I hated this.

I remembered the first time Oliver came over: mom

entertained with him my childhood photos while I got ready. By the time I made it to the living room, they'd been having the time of their lives, laughing at pictures of me playing naked in the sand on a beach. Sadly, I couldn't share in their joy because I felt like nothing had changed since then, except for my height, because the two cherry seeds that are my boobs, undeniably stayed the same. So, since the photo incident, I always felt a little uncomfortable whenever Oliver came over.

Mum liked Oliver because he reminded her of my dad in his youth.

So dad was also a little idiot, good to know!

Luckily this time, we skipped the photos and all the "look how much this little girl has grown" talk, although I don't think mum could have come up with anything new. Disregarding the photos and the fact that from now on, Oliver would always remind me of my dad, I was nonetheless glad that my parents liked him.

I was finally past the feeling that I'd rather be with Adam. Maybe the feeling was just gone, maybe I'd given up on him, or maybe I'd simply fallen in love with Oliver.

I wanted to be with him and leave that unfortunate period of my life behind.

Everything was covered in snow, so I had to keep both eyes on the road instead of Oliver. It would've been super lame if I'd slipped and fell in front of him. Oliver had the great idea to go sleigh-riding, but of course this was only a great idea to him.

Memories, those damned memories!

When I was little, my parents took me sleigh-riding with Ryan, the neighbor's son. He was a very violent little boy, but for some reason my parents really forced our "friendship." Mum wrapped me up in overalls and put the sort of beanie on my head that only leaves your nose free. I must have looked like a child version of the Michelin man. Because of that horrid kid, I had to ride on the back of the sleigh during our wonderful trip. Dad got so excited in his role as sleigh-puller, that he didn't even notice I'd fell off the sleigh. The demon child left me behind, hiding his evil laughter behind his mittens. Since the overalls were twice as big as me, I had no chance of surviving the ride. My arms flailed desperately in the snow and my tears fell in torrents. I was so scared that I'd never see my parents again, I couldn't stop yelling. Luckily, dad noticed my disappearance "quite soon" and eventually turned back for me. We never went sleigh-riding with Ryan again. Traumatized, it took years to overcome my fear of sleigh-riding and be able to sit on a sledge again.

In the end, we decided to walk but I had to explain to Oliver why I didn't want to have a sleighing evening. I recounted my little traumatizing episode to him and he had no further questions. But of course, he laughed at me. I'd have laughed too, if it hadn't happened to me. Eventually, we made it to the river bank, I kept my eyes mostly on the road, but I still stole a few glances at Oliver. Everything was frozen. It was a nice view and I could have enjoyed it more, if my hands weren't frozen.

I found out that Oliver's school was coming with us on the skiing trip, so we'd be able to spend the whole of next week together. It made the cold disappear, I didn't care about my icy nose anymore or the fact that I was frozen to the edge of the bench beside which we stood.

An awkward silence fell on us, the kind where you'd should say something to the other person, but your sentences avoid you, so you just stand there like an idiot, waiting for something to happen. But you don't say anything and, the moment to say something is gone. You move on and you'll never feel the same thing when your body and mind obviously urges you to move it on. Our moment wasn't lost because Oliver broke the silence.

"Are you cold? I can lend you my jumper."

Sure thing, hang another layer on me, I already have problems with moving in any other direction than straight ahead.

"That's very sweet of you but I already have a very cozy jumper," I said. *A cozy jumper? Really?* I can already feel the "Loser" sign lighting up on my forehead. A sad image flashed before my eyes: "Amy, 56, found dead, surrounded by her 999 ambivalent cats, wearing her self-knitted very cozy jumper and her extra warm knickers, while meticulously knitting her new fashion collection for the year 2050."

Oliver smiled about my "cozy jumper" or was it because he felt a bit embarrassed because this was our first meeting since our New Year's kiss. Since then, we hadn't had the chance to even discuss, finalize or at least admit what was really going on between us. You'd think saying "I love you" sorted everything out, but sometimes you still need a little push, something that can take it further for both sides.

"I wanted to talk to you about the *thing* that happened last time."

That *thing*? Does he consider saying, "I love you" just a *thing*, or is he calling *the kiss* a *thing*, or both?

"I've also wanted to talk to you about "the thing.""

"Really?" he looked at me, visibly relieved and smiled.

"Yeah, but you should start because you're the one who brought it up," I said firmly, trying to hide the fear that he'd disappear from one day to another like Adam did.

"I want to talk to you about what happened that night."

Why is he beating around the bush? A kiss and 'I love you', why can't he just say it?

"You mean 'what happened' when you kissed me and said that you loved me?" I asked with a bit more urgency, revealing my own emotions.

"No, that's not what I mean."

"Then what? I don't understand where you're going with all this."

"I mean, when you kissed me back and told me you loved me too. Was all that true?"

I was lost for words, yes it was my turn. I stood there embarrassed and I was afraid what would happen if I told him the truth.

"Yes," I finally said.

He hugged me and kissed me on the lips. His kiss warmed me so much I felt like I'd drunk ten mugs of hot tea in less than an hour. I wasn't cold anymore, at all. I didn't even need

95

all my layers of warm clothes anymore.

"I didn't know if you said it in the heat of the moment or if you really meant it. I don't know what's going on with us, so I wanted to talk to you about it. Amy, I'm so in love with you, that I don't even care about our friendship. I mean, I don't even care if we mess it up, I just want to be with you. For real. Officially, written on the sky, so that everybody knows."

Well, this must be what it's like when the moment doesn't go away. We had some special moments with Adam, but this with was different. With Adam I never knew what the next day might bring, with Oliver it was enough for me to know that he'd be there for me the following day as well. After a few more hours of walking, we went back to my house. Oliver left because he had to pick his little brother up from training.

Finally, a day when I could sleep in peace. Finally, the day had arrived when I'm dating a perfect boy like Oliver. My smile was glued to my face, so much so, that it almost bugged me to see my reflection grinning back at me while I brushed my teeth. I couldn't help it. I was finally happy. Mum and dad went to the cinema in the evening and invited me, but I chose to stay home. For once in my life, I wasn't filling my pillows full of tears. The second reason I didn't go with my parents was because I really wanted to finally perform my dance of joy.

Ruby texted me and asked if I was at home.

Alright, I'm willing to postpone my 'I'm finally dating a perfect boy' celebration for her.

I told her to come over and even invited her to sleepover if she felt like it. It'd been such a long time since we had a sleepover, anyway. She didn't answer immediately, which I interpreted as a yes, so I started preparing the essential elements of a girl's night in: mountains of crisps, mountains of chocolate, stacks of films and of course, I couldn't forget about the freshest issue of our favorite magazine because we always answered the personality tests together, with Ruby. However, while waiting for her I read some of the questions of the newest test: When will love find you? Of course I had to answer relevant questions like: "What color scarf do you wear when it rains?" or "If the sun is shining, but your BFF is depressed, where do you take her, to cheer her up?

The test predicted me that *love will soon knock on my front door*, but he's just left, so sorry favorite magazin of my life, you're not right this time.

Okay, I know I should've waited for Ruby to take the test, but I was so bored. Anyway, I answered the questions on a separate sheet of paper, so she wouldn't notice I'd already done it. It was as if nothing had happened.

The exact moment I threw my treacherous separate piece of paper in the rubbish, I heard a knock at the front door. *Finally*.

I slid into my monster-slippers and I shuffled to the door, but it wasn't Ruby who was standing there, it was Adam.

# Chapter Eight

Yes. He stood in my doorway. Him. He, who'd ripped my heart out and cut it into tiny pieces. He, who sucked away all my happiness and multiplied my tear producing ability. He, who I've fantasized about kicking in the ass for months. He, who I once loved. I didn't know what to feel or what to do that in this situation. He, stood before me with his perfect looks and suddenly my feelings for him weren't so easy to decipher.

Perfect looks, but imperfect personality.

Who does he think is, walking back into my life uninvited and unannounced, after destroying everything in my life that ever made me happy, on the very same day that I finally regained my happiness? Not to mention the fact that this time, with Oliver, my feelings and my happiness were finally reciprocated. Yes, Oliver loves me back and didn't abandon me when he felt like that.

"Amy, I know what you must think of me and where you'd like to send me, but please give me a minute so that I can explain my side of everything."

He thinks he knows where I'd want to send him? I sincerely doubt that. I think he has no idea what I actually think of him.

The worst thing was that I hated him whole heartedly. Honestly, I wanted to banish him to the deepest circles of hell and this scared me a bit. I shouldn't have felt anything, anything at all for him and yet.

Other people had such uncomplicated love lives, why couldn't I? Other girls meet a perfect boy, the boy fights for them and they live happily ever after, until one of them efs it up. What about me? I meet the perfect guy, I'm waiting for him to fight for me, but nothing happens. Then I catch myself chasing after him. Regardless of how much I fight for him, for us, he doesn't want me after all, end of story. Aaron used to mock me and call me The Ice Queen. But I didn't have ice in the place of my heart, actually my problem was that I was always melting for the wrong person.

I accidentally find someone who sweeps me off my feet, I do the same for him, we admit, "we've fallen for each other" and all of a sudden an evil little jerk like Adam turns up and tries to overshadow our happiness.

"I highly doubt, one minute would be enough. Plus, I don't have any time left to waste on you, anyway."

I wanted to slam the door in his face, but he blocked it with his hand.

"I fucked up. I shouldn't have left. I don't want anything else from you, but to apologize."

His voice was trembling and he had difficulty in forming the words.

My answer came out much more easily.

"Yep, you've interpreted the situation correctly. Now that you've apologized, we have nothing else to talk about. As far as your apology goes, you can stick it up there where the sun don't shine."

I slammed the door in his face.

He didn't knock again and he didn't come back. My neutral feelings for him were over, now I hated him even more than before, when he'd left. He had no right to come back and try to rewrite our story. The only thing he had to do was break down – *Check*- walk away – *yes, another Check* - and for me to stand up – *more or less, Check* – but that's it.

There's no next chapter or act for him, he doesn't deserve one.

I was furious when I went to sleep and when I woke up. I christened a puppet Adam and I spent the whole evening hurling my old textbooks at it, along with anything else I could find. The happiness I'd felt before Adam's arrival slowly returned, once one of the textbooks I'd launched at the puppet, seemingly knocked Adam out.

He comes here to apologize. Yeah, sure, pretend as if nothing happened, as if something hadn't started between us. I was really into him? Is this a joke?

I texted "Thanks a lot!" to Ruby because she'd forgotten to warn me about Adam's arrival. She must have known that we were bound to meet, but she hadn't said anything. I don't care if he'd just come from her house that minute, so she didn't have time to warn me. It was her sacred duty to let me know ahead of time. Yes, even if she had no idea Adam was in town because she was hanging out with Aaron. I can't be subjected to such shocks, especially not in my own home.

The school ski trip was fast approaching. Violet was the only one who decided to skip it because she was too behind with school stuff and the exam period was drew near. I was so thrilled about the skiing trip that I'd packed my luggage days before and readied my heart. It was the only place I could be together with Oliver as if Adam didn't exist. A place where he surely wouldn't find me.

Of course, this was all too good to be true. Although I was used to the fact that fate always has some special surprise planned for me, I somehow still believed that maybe, just this once it would find another victim instead of me.

The vast majority of students who were supposed to go on the ski trip were knocked out by a virus that had been infecting everyone in town, for weeks. Ruby and Aaron were out and to my great dismay my invincible Oliver too. All things considered, I didn't feel like going on the field trip at all, until I found out Tracy, a girl from our year, was still going. Tracy and I got along so well during school events, but for some strange reason we didn't keep in touch after them. I was happy that she was coming too and I didn't have to look at the stupid face of Cassie alone.

I offered to stay home with Oliver, but he was dead set against it. I went over to his place the weekend before going on the trip to say my tearful farewells and to double check if I'd packed everything for my long journey.

That's how it always goes: at home I'm convinced that I

have everything, but as soon as I leave I remember a million tiny things I'd forgotten. Last time, I was dumb enough to embark on a journey without my woolen hat. True, it's not like it was one of the most indispensable props to take on a ski trip. The main thing was to make sure I had was my eyeliner, which I'd double checked at least six times before leaving. Oh well... women.

Our group met at seven o'clock directly in front of the school building. Originally, we were supposed to go in two different buses, but since half of the group was sick, we only needed one. We always had two non-teacher adults with us, who were relatives of teachers or students, who took the duty upon themselves to keep problematic elements like Cassie at bay.

I texted Tracy the evening before to make sure that she was still coming. She reassured me that she was and offered to give me a lift to school. At 6:40 a.m. she waited in front of our house with her mum. I said goodbye to my parents and jumped into the car next to Tracy. On the way, we gossiped about Cassie and her crew. Surprisingly, Tracy didn't like them either. What a shocker! Tracy told me about Garrett, the boy she liked from the other school that was coming skiing with us. As it turned out, he was one of Oliver's friends. Of course, I promised her that I'd get all the possible info about Garrett. I was already texting Oliver about it when we arrived in front of the school. We said goodbye to her mum and joined the others. We loaded our stuff in the bus and set out to find ourselves a good seat. I checked twice where I put my bag because it'd already happened to me that I watched the bus drive away without my bag. I looked around, but I could barely see any familiar faces from my class, there were much more students from Oliver's year.

Miss Esther asked us to be quiet so she could give us the usual information about the field trip.

"If you have to use the toilette, please don't wait until we're in the middle of the highway, think of it while we're in a petrol station."

I never understood why she was always so careful with her

words. Just call a restroom a restroom, for goodness sake. I looked over at my travel companions, and highly doubted they understood her fancy language. But what could we do, our teacher was always this discreet. She never got straight to the point, only hinted at it. When she wanted quiet in her classroom, she worded it in a way, that made us laugh instead of shutting up. For example:

"I'd like to kindly ask the twittering students to chatter a bit more silently because knowledge won't enter your head on it's own accord."

Not a lot of students respected her because she was incapable of disciplining her students.

She always demanded silence, but she never got it. Nonetheless many students liked her.

The warning about the toilette inspired Tracy to go, right then because the next stop was in more than an hour. I fished out the Bestseller I'd bought specifically for this journey and dived in. The book was about two teenagers who'd been exchanging letters for years, but never met. They made a pact to be pen-pals for years and possibly meet each other one day, in person. It all seemed pretty absurd to me. For example, how would you know what the other one looked like? Okay, I know looks aren't everything. Well, that's a huge lie because with my history with boys, it's obvious that I think looks count more than anything else, considering the fact that I always go for the hot boys and it always ends in a catastrophe. Maybe I should reevaluate my own ways. Before I had the chance to get anywhere with the preface of the book, someone touched my shoulder.

"Hey, is this seat free?"

Dear Fate! I'd like to kindly ask you to forget about sending Adam back in to my life. It's a very bad joke.

"Sure thing. Once you sit down, the place next to it will be free too."

"Come on Amy, how long are you going to pretend to be angry at me?"

"Pretending? The only person who's into pretending is you."

I grabbed my bag and shoved it onto the seat next to me.

Where the hell is Tracy? Has she flushed herself down the loo, excuse me, the toilette? She could be the only one here, to save me from this embarrassing moment? I can't believe this! What the hell is he doing here? I hope he's not one of the accompanying adults!

My teacher answered my questions.

My illusions about being able to escape him were shattered. I had about ten minutes to decide if I'd join the others for the journey or run away either way, he would win!

I decided not to go anywhere. He should be the one going somewhere, for example to hell! I can't allow him to ruin my trip.

Tracy returned a little late.

"Oh my gosh, tell me that's not the Adam you've been telling me about!"

Sadly it was him.

"What is he doing here?" Tracy asked with disgust on her face.

"I guess he's writing the second part of his book and he hasn't scored the other girls," I answered ironically.

Tracy laughed which was a bit scary because I don't think it was that funny and we shouldn't forget the fact that I also walked into his trap.

People looked at us curiously when they heard our laughter, so I pretended that I was having the time of my life and was not at all disturbed by the presence of the blood sucker himself.

"Can I ask you something?" Tracy asked with puppy eyes.

"Sure, except if it's about him," I motioned towards Adam with a nod of my head.

Tracy rolled her eyes and decided not to ask me anything. I knew that she wouldn't let me be, so eventually, I gave in.

"Alright, ask away!"

I didn't have to say it twice because Tracy was already ready with her big question.

"So have your read his book?"

Maybe it was only obvious to me that after such a

misadventure with a vampire like Adam, any girl would've uttered malevolent incantations above his book, while she burnt it, threw it out or just tore it apart, page by page.

"No, I just tossed it out with the garbage."

Tracy laughed in her bizarre way, which attracted more and more attention from the others in the bus on us, so I tried to disappear into my bus seat.

"Have you never, not even in the smallest way been interested in the contents of the book?"

"I'm going to be brutally honest with you, Tracy. After he left, all I cared about was one question: Why? Why did he leave? Why was I such a loser that I believed all of his fake signs? Most of all: why didn't *the thing* that happened between us mean nothing to him? I'm not just talking about that one night, but all the others too, when nothing really happened but somehow it still did. I genuinely felt something and I know he did, too. At least I believed so."

"You never thought that the book might give you some answers?"

"After he'd left, I couldn't have cared less about his answers."

Tracy started to annoy me with her persistent book promotion and nagging questions. I felt like I was being interrogated:

Where were you the moment the tragedy of your abandoning happened? Tell us exactly what you have felt and how did you know your heart was broken.

"If you're so interested, you can read it for yourself. His book is coming out in February." I snapped at her.

"I'd surely be interested if a boy had written a book about me. To be honest, I'd be thrilled if anybody had written anything about me, you see what I mean?"

God, I guess in the end, I'll have to erect a memorial for him because he wrote a book about me And I should be grateful to him? Of course.

I got what Tracy meant, but I think we had very different opinions about these things. In her opinion, it was a big deal if someone wrote a book about you, or if someone was inspired by your presence. In my opinion, I was head over heels in love with Adam. I believed that he was going to be my husband and that we belonged together. I thought that the thing between us was sincere. He opened up to me and I opened up to him, even though I'd hated him in the beginning. He betrayed me, used me and didn't have any feelings for me, at least nothing as fairy tale-worthy as I felt for him. Bottom line is: he can go screw himself and his book.

The journey in the bus proved to be too long and the nearest petrol station seemed too far away. I was overthinking things. I always overthink everything. I shouldn't be ruminating about this or about anything that has to do with him.

I had to look for the answers in my own life and not some book. Maybe Oliver was the answer to everything, maybe not. Maybe there are no answers to anything, ever, at all. Maybe things just happen and no one will ever ask for our opinion about them. They happen and we can either learn to accept them and keep on living or we can get upset and continue living our life, while chasing away everyone who wonders into our path.

I don't want to live like that. Maybe that's the reason why Oliver came into my life and things happened the way they did. I don't know the reason why, but not even Oliver could change the fact that Adam was special to me.

I poked Tracy every five minutes, asking her if we were there yet. Why didn't I go to the "toilet" before leaving? It's again the fault of our resident jerk, who stole some valuable minutes from my life while the others went and relieved themselves.

After I got bored with counting the passing trees, I heard the sleepy voice of our teacher announcing that we were soon going to stop for a little break.

Oh, thank heavens! I was the first one to jump up from my seat and get off the bus when we finally arrived at our stop. I could still hear the teacher's comment which she intended to be funny, but I couldn't appreciate that much:

"Was somebody asleep when we had the chance to relieve

ourselves before leaving?"

Great, why don't you repeat it in the loudspeaker? Because people in the backseat might not yet be aware that I need to pee.

There was a rundown restaurant next to the petrol station, the crowd of students invaded it in the hope of using the restroom. We waited with Tracy for the crowd to disperse a bit then we passed time by investigating all the useless things for sale at the station, they had everything from key chains to cuddly toys.

The other students slowly left the restaurant while Tracy got so immersed in researching the goods that I decided to go in, alone.

I walked towards to the derelict building which had been ravaged by the tides of time. One of the letters on the restaurant board hung upside down. The lucky surviving letters were barely legible, but after some guesswork I figured the restaurant must be named *Joel & Beal*. I couldn't decide if it was designed to frighten people, or perhaps the owners just didn't care.

Once I entered, everyone turned to stare at me. Well that two people who were inside. One of them was the waiter, the other the serial-killer-looking customer disguised as a truck driver. Needless to say, he was pretty creepy. He wore a tattered red T-shirt and a weathered red baseball cap.

At least he's got some fashion sense.

He had a huge scar on his face making him look even more like a character from some terrifying horror movie.

Amy! Why the hell have you watched all those horror movies? Why?

I was alone, without Ruby who would at least have been my partner in fear. Tracy was still nowhere to be seen, swallowed by the flood of the store's useless stuff.

"Good morning," I whispered to the two people staring at me.

Why did I have to come in here alone? Why didn't I just join the others? Why do I always get myself into situations like this? I'm scared. Oh, come on, Amy, start walking!

I headed towards the restroom with slow, careful steps. I hoped the others wouldn't be massacred by the time I was finished. That's how the horror films always started, there was the main loser (in this case, me) and the other insignificant losers. Actually, I think they're the lucky ones because they die first, while the others naively believe they have a chance. As the main loser, I'd have to suffer ninety minutes until finally, hunted down. Okay, ninety minutes on the big screen, sometimes it lasts longer in real life, but my point is that I'd certainly suffer longer than anyone else by the time the main villain (in the tattered t-shirt) offs me.

I solemnly swear that I will never watch a horror film again, if I survive this trip and get back home safely. Never, never, never!

I went to the restroom and stopped in front of the mirror. I'm not sure exactly, what happened to me, but I had a very bad feeling. I hoped they wouldn't lock me in here and then tie me up. I hoped I'd have a chance in this life and that... Suddenly there was a knock on the door.

"Who's that?" I asked, voice trembling with fear.

"Your worst nightmare."

Well, he wasn't very far from the truth, but if someone had ever told me in these past few months that I'd be happy to hear that voice, I'd have slapped them.

"What do you want?" I asked in relief, but still showcasing that I still didn't love him.

"I just wanted to let you know that we're leaving, soon. But if you want to stay here forever, that's fine too."

"No, I'm coming just a second."

"Are you okay?"

How could I be okay, there's a serial killer outside the door, haven't you seen him?

"Sure, but..." *if anybody asks, I'd deny ever having said this*: "could you wait for me?"

Silence. I guess he was standing there with a victorious smile on his face.

"Sure."

I plucked up my courage and stepped outside. I felt a bit

calmer knowing that I wouldn't walk past the scary, scar-faced truck driver alone. I wasn't afraid, but I placed one foot after the other more confidently with Adam by my side.

"Hey, you there, stop for a second!" a rough voice, thick from decades of smoking called after us.

I didn't dare turn around, my legs started shaking. Adam noticed and pushed me behind his back, then took my hand.

"You are afraid."

"I am not."

"I can see that you're shaking."

"Well, you aren't seeing it correctly. If I was afraid, I would be giving you another chance to protect me and honestly, I don't want to. Look at me, I'm not even trembling anymore."

"I would want you to shiver because I'm ready to protect you again."

"That's the difference between us, I'm not here for you to walk all over me, again."

Adam turned around and gave the truck driver a questioning look.

"You've forgotten this." The smokey-voiced truck driver said.

"That's my woolen hat, my hat!" I cried out. "Thank you so much!" I said blushing, while I counted my blessings that we weren't actually victims in a horror movie.

On the way out, we stopped holding hands and kept a walking distance of a few steps between us. Before we got on the bus, Adam turned to me.

"You were afraid."

"I wasn't afraid, I just wasn't very brave."

Returning to the others, Tracy noticed right away that I arrived with my nemesis. The only thing she asked me, was if I was okay. I said yes, although nothing was actually *okay*. Especially not me. What was so special about him? Nothing. So please tell me how could he crawl into my head and set up camp there.

# Chapter Nine

In an attempt to stop thinking about him, I started reading my book again, but I got nowhere fast, with it. I saw him on every page: in the characters, the plot, the names, the letters, I could insert him everywhere, even if he had nothing to do there – just like in my life.

For some reason he was still a perfect match for me.

I sat on the bus in silence and I could see myself from the outside. I even saw what I didn't want to see. I felt as if I had been in some kind of lame comic. The problem was simple: there were no superheroes in this comic, just some lame guy who always managed to hurt me, a lot.

Garrett, Tracy's new crush sat two seats in front us. Tracy did her best to catch his eyes, but didn't really succeed because Garrett kept staring out of the window. Tracy kept looking at his headrest, hunting for the perfect occasion. The perfect occasion for Garrett to turn, for their eyes to meet and for both of them to realize they belonged together. However, Garrett was hopeless. He didn't even turn when Shane and Will were almost killing each other in the back seats.

On the other hand, someone who nobody wanted to see kept looking back at us the whole time. I wish I knew why.

Oliver called me twice, but I couldn't have a normal conversation with him above all the noise on the bus. I managed to get that Garrett was single, but he didn't know if he was ready to mingle. He suggested that Tracy should wait for him to make the first move because he didn't like demanding girls.

Every boy says this, but in most cases if you just wait to be noticed by them, then you'll stay invisible and wind up watching your crush hook up with an easy girl. Yeah. Let's think back to what happened with Cassie and Adam. I really doubt, Adam had to chase after *Ms. The Moment I See A Hot Guy, My Thighs Fly Wide Open.*

We quickly discarded the idea of Tracy going to the front to ask how much we have left

from the journey and on the way back she accidentally falls into Garrett's arms pretending that the bus driver stepped on the break violently.

It was too obvious and too difficult to believe. We needed a craftier master plan and fortunately, we had a whole week to come up with it.

Soon Miss Esther stood up and announced the good news, we'd soon arrive. Thank God! Will and Shane had driven me mad with their immature jokes. Of course, it's possible that someone else would find them hilarious for throwing pieces of paper in Lauren's hair while the poor girl slept as innocently as a baby.

A few minutes later the bus passed the familiar billboard.

Welcome to the paradise of ski slopes. Ye who enter here abandon all hope of leaving without a broken limb. Have fun!

Very encouraging words for those of us who are here for our first time.

Luckily, I lost my "leg breaking, virginity" during my first ski trip, so now I felt sort of safe, unlike Tracy who had so far, always managed to survive without any injuries.

As we arrived to the accommodation, Tracy headed for our favorite cabin. It was suddenly strange to me, that every year, we've spent the entire ski trip together, but didn't really talk to each other afterwards. I was always too busy with my best friend or my usual heartbreak. In any case, I didn't know why I never paid more attention to Tracy.

We chose the room we liked the most while everyone else entertained each other in the hall. I was so relieved we got Holly and Ruth as roommates and not Cassie and her gang.

Inside our room we found the usual bunk beds. I hated

them. If I chose the lower bunk, I was terrified that the upper bunk would crash down and kill me. If I chose the upper bunk, I was afraid that I'd fall off during the night and break every bone in my body. I remembered the first time that we came here. I took the mattress from the lower bunk and slept on the floor. There, I only risked an insect attack, which was something I could survive.

Holly and Ruth were a strange pair of twins. Oliver had already told me about them, they were the cool girls in his school. Everybody wanted to be like them, everybody wanted to be their friends, but they never let anyone get too close to them. It was impossible to access their secret society which only had two members, strictly. I was pretty surprised they even came on this trip loaded with people.

Considering my current predicament, however, I preferred to be with the two weirdos than the girl who had smeared the lips of my ex-love. We started unpacking when Tracy poked me to look out the window.

It was Adam heading towards the slope with his snowboard under his arm.

Judging from all the noise outside, I deduced that Garrett's classmates were drooling over Adam.

"I think he could title his new book: Help! I don't remember which jerk I hooked up with during the last ski trip!"

Tracy giggled and surprisingly, even Holly and Ruth smiled. They exchanged a secret look then Ruth turned to me:

"Do I guess correctly that you two are together?"

"No way! Adam's a disrespectful idiot!"

Tracy tried to signal to Ruth, drop the topic. I pretended not to see her reflection in the window.

I hated seeing him, here. I hated that I had to think of him. I hated that I couldn't think of anything else except him. Most of all, I hated the graceful way he maneuvered down the slope, my lust for him almost killed me. He was too perfect, it seemed simply impossible for him to mess anything up, except for the two of us. Honestly, he'd still look good even if he tumbled. I hated him even more.

I desperately missed Oliver and my recent life when I was officially over Adam. Everything was so unpretentious with Oliver. I tried not to think of him – I mean Adam. But it wasn't that simple. I tried to drive him out of the sea of my thoughts into new waters, preferably into a waterfall where he would drown and disappear in a matter of a few seconds so I could be myself, again. I'd also be fine with an avalanche burying him or a huge yeti teaching him an overdue lesson, but sadly the chances for all this weren't very high. I'd tried everything I could except for one thing: accepting the fact that I'd never be my old self again and that maybe somewhere deep down, I still wasn't over him.

There was a knock on the door. Tracy opened it and a giant silence followed. Holly and I simultaneously turned around. Garrett stood in the doorway explaining something about a party in the evening. Tracy was so embarrassed, that Holly had to come to her rescue. When Garrett was out of ear range, Tracy started babbling.

"Did you hear all that? Garrett just invited us to a party. He actually acknowledges my existence?"

None of us ever understood Tracy's lack of confidence because she was extremely pretty. She was different from the likes of Cassie, because she didn't sleep with everyone right away and she was also intelligent. Although Tracy wasn't aware of it, I knew for certain that lots of boys in our school wanted to date her, but they didn't dare ask her out because they thought she was way out of their league.

I gave Garrett a fleeting glance. He had longish, dark-brown hair with a sort of toned body. (I'm saying "sort of" because under his baggy grandma jumper, I couldn't really discern if it was muscle or yet another layer of clothes.) He was quite a handsome guy and I could easily have imagined him with Tracy by his side.

She was so deep into the Garrett talk with Ruth, that the other girl confessed she'd been into Garrett's friend for a while, but it's unrequited because Jed was supposed to have a girlfriend. Holly had been in a happy relationship for three years so she didn't take part in our high-brow discussions.

I wrapped myself in silence because I also had a boyfriend at home. Yes, Oliver. Oliver and not Adam.

Tracy was completely beside herself with the thought of the party. She changed outfits six times, told us that she'd stay in our room seven times and even asked us (at least ten times) if we really thought, she had a chance with Mr. Knitted Jumper. I didn't want to discourage her by telling her that the only possible explanation for Garrett not being into her could be that he's actually into guys. His soapy face and knitwear made him very suspicious.

Ruth and Holly didn't behave at all like the image Oliver had painted of them. Holly was more mature than her twin sister and us, for that matter, but it was alright because Holly was brainy and always positive.

I was full of question marks when I set out for the party. Of course, I was fuelled by the ancient desire to make Adam's heart sink when he sees me and to prompt the realisation that he was an idiot when he'd left me. On the other hand, I was theoretically over him, so I really had no reason to entertain such childish matters. Of course, in the end, my childish self triumphed and I dolled up like all the other girls.

"It's not a sin to want a bit of revenge," Holly told me quietly, while Ruth and Tracy tried to do something with their hair.

Her words stayed with me. True, how could it be a sin to get pretty for a party just like my friends? Maybe because I had a boyfriend who was a very nice guy? I wasn't doing anything sinful just because I refused to wear rags.

If we have to be honest, in a place where the temperature is constantly below zero, it's quite difficult to go anywhere and stay pretty without carefully applied make-up freezing on our face.

I wore a black dress that managed to hide my pair of tights I pulled all the way up to my neck, to keep from getting cold.

Miss Esther came knocking on everybody's door to tell us that a huge snow storm was expected and everybody should remain in their own bedrooms.

Of course, Miss! After we all got ready, we waited ten

minutes listening for Miss Esther's to go upstairs then we sneaked out from our building and headed over to the other building that Garrett invited us to party in.

The weather outside was pretty rough, but nothing could stand in the way of our getting to that party. When we arrived everybody stared at us. Garrett stood at the staircase and motioned for us to follow him. We arrived to the secret location of the secret party.I almost turned back at the door, but Holly grabbed my hand.

Adam leaned against a table, talking with Jed.

"What the hell is he doing here?" I whispered angrily to Holly and shot an angry glance towards Adam.

"I don't know, but his eyes are almost falling out of their sockets since you entered the room."

Good! That's what they should fall out so that he can't annoy me with them.

I hated his presence, because it always reminded me of the special feeling I'd only had with him. But I didn't want to feel like this. Not for him. I was happy and sad at the same time.

Cassie and company sat in the corner in their usual party pose. They had their arms crossed while they gossiped about everybody who walked past them, then they'd lean back, feeling fortunate that they are who they are. Their only problem was that they didn't realize everyone else pitied them, rather than envied them.

I didn't want to feel Adam's eyes on me, but I did. I didn't want to look in his direction, but I felt like we were the only ones in the room. I stayed with Holly, while Ruth and Tracy tried to low-key ensnar their victims. Garrett was glancing more and more often in Tracy's direction. Even Holly noticed it and we agreed that if they ended up together Tracy should buy Garrett a better jumper before someone beats him up for his lack of fashion sense.

As I watched them, I realized they'd really make a good couple one day. Garrett was like a boy version of Tracy. They were shooting furtive glances towards each other until occasionally their eyes met and one of them immediately looked away. It was pretty funny to watch from the outside as the same thought shined in the eyes of both of them: "I like you."

Holly went to call her boyfriend and I stayed alone with the party animals. I tried to pretend that Adam wasn't there, as if he didn't even exist. People seemed to be having a good time so I just watched them. It was nice to watch something being born in front of my eyes. Everyone had a reason to be happy except for me. I did have a reason to be happy though didn't I? Oliver. At that instant, I should have gone back to my room because I'd promised Oliver that I'd call him tonight. Tracy who normally never drank (like seriously, never ever drank) now was drinking and started to ease up in Ruth's company. I glimpsed my sour face in a passing mirror, I knew I needed to go home. I said goodbye to my friends and made my way outside. Holly caught up with me in the staircase, grabbed my arm and pulled me in her direction.

"Where are we going?" I asked.

"I want to show you something."

I didn't know what she wanted, but I followed her into the room under the stairs.

"Where are we?"

"Amy, this is Adam's room and now we're going to do what you should have done for ages."

She made me sit on the bed and pushed a book in my hand.

"No, no way!"

"Read it. I'll stand guard to make sure nobody comes in."

"I don't care about this rubbish and anyway, I wouldn't finish it in so little time, even if I wanted to. And let me be clear, I don't want to."

"Leaf through it, take photos with your phone, I don't care what you do, but do something."

Holly was behaving like Ruby would. I didn't understand why she cared so much about me, it was nice. I stared at her, confused.

"Why?" I asked.

She smiled.

"Amy, you're in love. It's fine as long as you know who is

115

on the receiving end of it. I'm not going to say anything else about my guess. I haven't had the chance to tell you my story and it's not why we came here, I just want to solve yours. If we have a little time, I'll tell you everything and then you'll understand why I insisted."

I didn't understand the situation or Holly, but for some reason, I was certain that she was right, I had to get to the end of this story. And once I get to the end of it, I'll put a full stop to all of it, so that it'll really finally be over.

I opened the book somewhere in the middle. The answers were waiting for me here, so I decided to dive right in.

*I can't bear her much longer.*

What?

"She was just as empty as all the others. She reminded me of my mistakes in the past. She was chatting about stupid things all the time and she wouldn't have shut up even if I'd paid her. The most difficult part was to pretend to kiss her because I wanted to kiss someone else: the girl who was driving me crazy. The girl who I found just as annoying as she was attractive. It upset me that for the first time in my life I couldn't see through someone, it annoyed me because for the first time in my life I felt like I was really interested in someone."

Pretending? My heart's eyes started vibrating in a strange way and it felt like someone had thrust a huge knife in my heart. A mistake? You were the biggest mistake in my life, matey.

# Chapter Ten

His lines tore at my heart and his words burnt through every cell in my body. Was I really so horrible that kissing me felt like a torture? My face went red. I felt dizzy. Okay, clearly I wasn't over him. My delusions of walking away with my head up high no matter what happened, were over. I hung my head so low that my nose almost touched the floor. I hated him with every fiber of my being.

Holly had a foot in the door and tried to listen closely for anyone approaching. My throat was besieged by little lumps, the forerunners of crying. I inhaled deeply twice and started crying on the third one. Holly ran to me and gave me a hug. I didn't say anything just placed the book in her lap.

"Tear it out," Holly said quickly.

"No way!"

"Bring the whole thing then, I refuse to believe that this is all there is."

Holly was completely besides herself and I got the impression that she was really sympathizing with me. I placed the book on the table and walked out. Holly ran back, tore out two pages and pushed them in my hand.

"Why did you do that? We're going to get busted."

"If it's really about you, I'll volunteer to tell him that I was the one who tore out the pages. I'll also beat him up for you."

As a matter of fact, the other girls were right, I did find answers to my questions in those pages. He left because he didn't feel anything for me. He loved a girl who wasn't me.

It's okay, I'll get over it one day. If not sooner than later. Maybe in ten years, maybe even later, but the day will come when I won't care about him, no matter what he does.

We were just about to leave when I spotted Adam and Jed walking towards their room. The room in which we were trespassing.

"Holly, we have a problem."

We exchanged glances then looked at the closet and the bed.

"Alright, you're smaller, so you go into the closet and I'm going under the bed," Holly ordered.

"What do I do if they want to change? Do I hand them their clothes?"

"And what will you do, clever girl, if they walk in through the door? You'll tell them that we were trying to find answers in Adam's book, to the question of why he's such an idiot?"

We didn't have time to discuss anything else because just before the door opened I managed to crawl into the closet as Holly squeezed herself under the bed. Once inside, I remembered a very important piece of information: I was allergic to dust. I only survived because I thought of the fact that somewhere in the world, let's say under the bed, there was another girl, let's call her Holly, who must have felt similarly unfortunate.

The boys walked in the room, Jed was in the middle of a tirade about his girlfriend. I held two pages of Adam's book in my hand. One of them fell on top of his shoes. I reached out for it carefully and by the dim light that filtered through the creeks I was able to read it:

"I saw how she looked at him. I saw that with him she was different than with me. With him she seemed calm and maybe even happy. What could I give her? I've never been happy in my life, could I make anyone happy? I learnt to let go, to exclude people and I'm not ready yet to let someone in. But she managed to break through my defenses.

You know you and me will never be indifferent to each other. It doesn't matter if there is someone else, and I'm sure there will be someone else, for you and maybe also for me. Maybe one day I'll get over you and the fact that I screwed

118

things up. Maybe with time I will be able to forgive myself for messing it up. However, don't say that we were indifferent for each other, because it's not true. You don't have to love me, you don't have to tolerate me, you don't have to understand me or riddle our relationship out because it took me a long time as well. The only thing I know for sure is that we're going to meet again one day. Farewell!"

So Cassie is the love of his life or god knows what other bitch. My fury was somewhat mitigated by the fact that I was hiding in a closet waiting for any miracle that would get me out of there without Adam and Jed noticing. Holly had a better hiding place than me. Well maybe not better, but definitely more spacious.

Jed was babbling on and on. He was just sprouting words like there was no tomorrow. It was horrible! I'd always believed that boys overthought things less than girls did, but Jed managed to prove the contrary.

"Hey, listen," Jed said after a thirty minute long monologue. "Has something like this ever happened to you before?"

"Like what?" asked the other IQ champion.

"That you were with someone while secretly you wanted to be with somebody else?"

Well, I can answer that one for him. Of course it has happened to him! Hey, one of his victims is sitting right here in the closet. We were together, well that wasn't quite true, but something else was going on. When our love should have come into full bloom, he just left deceitfully. Now, I found out from his cheesy writing that he also wanted someone else just like you did, my dear disgusting Jed.

"Well, it happened a bit differently with me, but something similar happened to me. I think you should just tell her what you feel."

Is he for real? Giving people romantic advice. I couldn't believe my ears. He, who had not enough courage to stand in front of me, look me in my eyes and tell me that we were over, is now giving advice about relationships to someone

119

else? Is this a joke?

They'd been talking for a while when Jed finally confessed who it was about.

"I wish our situation was easier! She also has someone, just like me. This thing between us has been going on since we started school, but it's going nowhere. She's toying with me and I let her. She'll never leave her boyfriend and maybe that's how it should be. I know that what I'm doing is not right, but I can't stop it. I just can't forget her."

When I heard the girl's name, I put my hands in front of my mouth to prevent any sound from escaping. He was talking about Holly! I ran through the things I'd already known: Ruth had been into Jed for a while. Jed had been secretly hooking up with Holly, who was in a relationship just like Jed was. And by the way, Holly was still hiding under the bed, listening to all of their conversation just as I was.

My nose was started itching. No way! It wasn't yet time for me to get busted. I had to sneeze and I panicked. I pulled one of the nonchalantly crumpled jumpers to my face. I had no idea if it was Adam's or Jed's, I didn't care. I hated both of them.

Please let me get out of here. I promise I'll be good, I'll become a better person. I won't wish for anything bad for Adam, Dylan or any other jerks that have broken my heart. Also, I won't call them bad names. I'm sure they are all good people at the bottom of their hearts.

It was too late, I sneezed. I wish I could tell you it was discreet, but it wasn't. The boys heard me.

"What was that?" Jed asked and then they both looked towards the closet. I felt their eyes on me so intensely that I was sure they could've opened the closet door with their gaze alone.

"We have an expected visitor," Adam said laughing.

I knew our accidental spying mission would end soon and I'd die of humiliation. They'd open the door and the earth would swallow me, but then I saw Holly come out from under the bed and she started shouting at Jed.

"You can't like me! If you want to like someone, like Ruth."

Jed and Adam stared at Holly who didn't seem embarrassed at all by the fact that she'd just crawled out from under their bed like it was completely normal.

Holly's counter strike was so successful that the boys forgot about me. Adam left the room saying that they should discuss this between the two of them. *Really? Make it three.* After having patiently listened to Holly's tirade, Jed stepped in front of her:

"I like *you* and not Ruth. To be honest, I feel like something has changed. It might have started out as a game, but it has become more – at least for me. You could deny it, but there is no need. I can see the difference when you look at me and when you look at him. Something is not like it used to be. You would want him to pay attention to you, to love you. I used to love you, but you didn't want me. Then, I knew this thing was never real between us, so I had to move on. I couldn't live with the thought that I was the only one feeling all this. I'm not the one for you, so this must end even if you are the one for me. I sound like an idiot and it hurts like hell. I wouldn't have thought that a heart could break even when you're doing something good. You need to heal your relationship and I need to let you do it. I'll close mine and move on. It started as a game, but I'm no longer enjoying playing it."

I realized a few things sitting there, in the closet: First, if you're sitting somewhere in an uncomfortable position, let's say in a closet, hugging your knees for more than half an hour, you can easily have pins and needles in your feet. Second, you only realize this when you are finally out of there. Third, while you're at it, you should figure out what you're going to say to everyone outside the closet when you realize you can't stay hidden in your closet forever.

Holly started crying, Jed stood before her not knowing what to do. He pulled her closer and held his breath, trying not to cry.

I'd like to further elaborate on my previous list.

Fourth, Jed was in love with Holly. Fifth, Holly was in love with Jed, but because of her sister and boyfriend, she kept it a secret even from herself. Sixth, I was now in possession of information I had no business of knowing, so I was done with hiding in closets.

Holly looked at Jed then said quietly:

"Maybe you're right. I loved him and for a long time I would have killed for him to love me. I gambled, I lost. Yes, I have Ruth but I could never look in her eyes again. If she figured it all out, she'd never talk to me again. Do you understand? Never! You're wrong about one thing though: I could never look at my boyfriend like I looked at you, that's why I've lost, because I've fallen in love with you."

Holly's voice broke. Jed took his hand.

"It's going to be as you wish."

Holly asked him to go back to the party and Jed followed him silently.

Oh, and I almost forgot, Holly saved me from complete embarrassment.

The coast was finally clear, I crawled out of the closet. I barely felt my legs, it took me a few minutes until I could use them again.

How will I look in Holly's eyes? Can't we pretend that I haven't heard anything? What about Ruth?

I looked around before I stepped out of the door, but luckily no one was there. There was such an intense snow storm raging outside that the elderly receptionist, Steve, asked me not to go out. Of course, I ignored the warning of someone older and wiser, because naturally, a teen girl knows better than anyone else. The storm almost blew me away, but at that moment I felt the wind might actually do me a favor by getting rid of me. The wind did blow away my woolen hat. I fumbled around in the dense snow, trying to find it. I couldn't see anything. I had no idea how to get back to our lodging because all the possible trails back were covered in snow. I tried to imagine that if I started from the left then I'd probably head right because that's where our cabin was. Just straight ahead. My feet were completely frozen and I couldn't see the top of our cabin. I started crying.

I remembered the time when I was small and my parents lost me in the zoo and I stood there alone and thinking about what would happen if I never saw them again. I was afraid that someone else would take me home, that I'd never sleep in my own bed again and I'd never see Ruby either. After the incident at the zoo, I was a little angel for a week. Of course after the week passed, I was back to normal, but still.

I spotted my hat and I grabbed it. It was completely soaked along with my tights. Suddenly someone put their arm around my shoulder. I couldn't see anything other than an arm that pulled me up from the snow covered ground and towards themselves.

"Are you alright? What has gotten into you, going out in such a miserable weather?"

"I don't know what happened. I just…"

"You just what? Try to think a little bit, please!"

I felt weird. It was Garrett. The realization clawed into my heart so violently that I almost collapsed. I wouldn't admit it, even to myself but at that moment, I'd wanted Adam not Garrett to have rescued me. I wanted him to pull me closer, chide me, take care of me.

Garrett grabbed my hand and led me back to my cabin. We walked for fifteen minutes in the storm and silence. When we finally got back to our building I cleaned the snow off myself and thanked Garrett for finding me. He looked at me and said:

"Don't thank me."

He motioned towards the door and then disappeared. Adam stood there, visibly worried. He came up to me and sat down.

"Are you okay?"

"Yes," I answered.

"Alright, then I'm off."

He stood up as if it was the most natural thing in the world that he'd been worried about me and headed out.

"Adam, wait!"

He turned around and looked at me.

"Yeah?"

"I just wanted to say thank you."

He didn't say anything just walked towards me. He stopped directly in front of me and caressed my messy hair away from my face.

"Yeah, you have many things to thank me for."

His answer didn't surprise me for a minute. Cynicism was as much his signature move as mine. His smile disappeared as he traced my chin with his index finger.

"Are you aware that we're standing underneath the mistletoe?"

I pushed his hand away and searched his eyes.

"Are you aware that it only counts during Christmas time which is now over, just like us?"

He smiled, then leaned closer to my lips.

"Did you figure that out sitting in the closet? Or should I say bless you?"

He knows!

"What closet?"

Of course, I didn't think for a moment that I could convince him otherwise. He stopped and gazed into my eyes again. His lips were almost touching mine. I tried to push him away with one hand, but I didn't succeed. In my other hand, I tried to hide the unread pages I'd torn out from his book. It was time for me to tell him that I knew about the other girl and how much he loved her.

Thinking back, I realized I'd felt something deeper than hate for him, at that moment. Reading those lines really hurt me, I was jealous of that girl who he loved so much, even if it was Cassie. It hurt that I was just a distraction for him. Why wasn't I the main event?

What does a girl do in this case? Of course, she decides to withhold any further feelings instead of confessing her real feelings for him:

"I have someone."

He was still admiring my lips when he answered.

"I'm well aware."

On the third try, he gave in and let me push him away. Maybe he suddenly understood the weight of what I said, maybe I just had as well. After Adam had abandoned me, I had a choice: I could get stuck in the emotional turmoil he caused and wait for him to come back or I could start again. I chose to move on and I did this for a reason. It was nice being with Oliver, but if I kept repeating this mantra rather than dealing with the realization that had been haunting me since Adam's return would hurt even more. I felt good with Oliver, but he wasn't Adam and he could never be Adam. Sometimes we have to let go off someone we really want to be with, because they no longer belong to us or because we belong to someone else.

Adam said goodbye and walked towards another bedroom. I stood silent for a while, until I managed to gather myself and walk in the right direction. Away from Adam.

I barely had time to sulk in bed because Holly exploded into the room with so much intensity, I thought someone had been attacked.

"Amy, listen to me, please! I can only imagine what you must be thinking of me and you're right. To be more exact, I hope you're not thinking the things I'm thinking about myself at the moment. I'm disgusting and so are the things I have done. My relationship with Larry hasn't been ideal for a while, but I was unable to handle the situation like an adult woman should. My reason for this is simple: I'm not at all an adult woman, I'm just on my way to becoming one. Once, I loved Larry but after Jed came into my life, everything changed. Everything was so different with him, it all so easy that I didn't even understand it. I didn't want to impress him, I didn't want to prove a point to him, I just wanted to enjoy being myself and being loved for who I am. I was so blind, that I hadn't realized that Larry and I were never on the same wavelength even though, I was with him for three years because I was afraid to leave him. I didn't know that a different type of relationship existed, like the one I had with Jed."

Holly told me everything from the very beginning. On one hand, I completely understood her, on the other I felt really sorry for Ruth. I promised Holly that I would keep quiet, but I tried to nudge her to confess to her sister. It would be much worse if Ruth heard it from someone else, for example, Jed. Who knows? Men are unpredictable, even when they're just little boys who might become men one day.

Holly and I talked almost all night long. She decided that she'd let Jed go and try to start again, alone. I didn't quite agree with her decision but since I've gone through the same thing, I mean the big decision of *I'm going to forget him*, multiple times before, I just nodded. I gave her and her attempt at closing it off with Jed one week.

It would be so nice if it was really that simple. I just say it's over and I don't love him anymore and my feelings take their stuff and climb out of my heart, while I continue living my life as if he'd never existed. And yet I wished many times that the feelings should stay with me because who knows if I'm ever going to have the chance to feel the same for someone else. Other times, I just wish I'd never met him.

Having let out all her tears, Holly looked at me with puffy eyes.

"What was written on the pages?"

Compared to hers, my problem seemed insignificant. She'd have to get out of a three year long relationship, while I'd just need to let Oliver make me happy and forget Adam ever existed, as I've done once before.

I cut her monologue short by telling her, he was actually writing about Cassie, something I'd need to digest, but I'd manage.

Holly didn't understand Adam and she was unwilling to let it go.

"Amy, I owe you a confession: I've seen you with Adam."

I didn't know how to react since nothing happened.

"I've been in this situation," she said.

"What situation?" I asked, like it was nothing to me that I'd almost completely crumbled because of Adam's presence.

"This turning up out of nowhere stunt. He always appears as if nothing's even happened, he just stands in front of you, as irresistible as he did before he left. You try your best to stay angry at him, you try to recall all the misery you felt the last time he left, but nothing changes. Everything stays the same and you love him just the same."

"I don't really understand. Jed was there for you all along, wasn't he?"

"Jed is Jed. He was there when I called him, but he never came on his own accord. Now he tells me that he loves me, but will he feel the same tomorrow? He always finds me interesting for a while, but what happens when the magic fades? Will he still love, if I'm not unattainable? Jed is such a child. I toyed with him because I had to, but I have no idea what would happen if this *thing* becomes more than it already is? If it turns into something important, if I change or he changes. Now that it's happened."

I managed to calm Holly down and didn't say a word about that one page from the jerk's book which I hadn't read yet. Anyway, we waited up for Ruth and Tracy and then we all went to sleep.

Next day was supposed to be an all-day skiing extravaganza. Learning from the snowstorm the night before, I paid much more attention to my warm clothing and didn't care if I looked like a pregnant snow(wo)man.

I had some challenges when it came to skiing. I sucked at it. Every year, Miss Esther divided us into two groups, I was always in the beginner one and spent my entire day struggling with my other clumsy group mates. This year was no different.

Miss Esther asked the usual questions like who has ever skied before. This was always one of the easiest questions to answer because I had skied before. Of course, we can't forget the fact that every year, I am somehow given skis that are in such bad shape, they make me super clumsy on the slopes.

It's not my fault at all, it's the skis, those cursed skis!

Lots of people raised their hands when she asked who'd never skied before, in their lives. She then added that all those people who raised their hands would practice skiing with Adam.

No, no way! Panic attack Act II, curtains call! The last thing I need in my life is for Adam to show me how to put one foot after the other. No way!

I signed up for the advanced group although I was well aware that I had no chance of getting out of this adventure uninjured. Faced with the choice of stumbling around in front of Adam or possibly physically injuring myself with the others, I choose the second one, hands down. *I'm not that clumsy anyway. I just have to go down a slope, what's the big deal? I've managed to do it every year, so far. I can do it this year too!*

By the time I thought it over a sixth time, I felt like I might have made the wrong choice.

Holly was also in the advanced group, while Ruth and Tracy chose to join the beginners. I was about to go with the other group when Adam called Miss Esther aside. After a few seconds Miss Esther modified her announcement.

"We're going to change things up, but don't worry. Trevor is going to take just as good care of our beginners as our champion, Adam would have."

What champion? What Adam? I can't believe this!

I shot a terrified glance at Holly who smiled back at me, cool as a cucumber.

"But he is not into you, right?" Holly asked, giving Adam a cynical glance.

"Holly, we have a problem," I said, my voice trembling.

"I know, but don't worry, we're going to ice this problem very soon."

"No, it's a much bigger problem."

"What can be a bigger problem than an arrogant idiot pretending not to die of the desire to be with you?"

"Well, honestly. How about the fact that I can't ski."

"What?"

Holly broke out in a fit of laughter and everybody stared at us. Holly was literally dying of laughter and I tried to hide my shame by pulling my woolen hat over my face.

"I hope you're aware that it would be extremely embarrassing to change groups now?"

"If I weren't aware, I wouldn't be panicking!"

Holly couldn't stop laughing while everyone in the advanced group stared at us.

"Is everything alright, girls?" Adam looked in our direction with a sarcastic smile on his face. I was ninety-nine percent sure he wanted to witness my clumsiness with his own eyes.

Holly shouted back that everything was peachy and we joined the others.

I'll survive, I'll survive, there will be no problems at all.

I lined up next to Holly and off we went. I had no problems with putting on the skis. Adam gave us a funny introductory course about the secrets of skiing. The wider your $V$ is, the more you're breaking. If you want to accelerate, try to get your $V$ as tight as possible. Although, he added, he was sure that everyone already knew this. He looked at me and I looked away quickly.

His words were followed by laughter from the other boys in our group. Will and Shane thought of something else to add and of course couldn't help but voice their wonderful opinions.

We lined up in front of the ski lift where I kept nudging Holly to come up with something because I was sure that I wouldn't be able to go down the slope without problems. She insisted that riding the ski lift, was the easiest thing in the world. I would've believed her if I didn't already know that I was the clumsiest person on the slopes.

I got into the lift and when I looked beside myself I saw, to my horror, that Adam had got in next to me and not Holly. I turned back in panic for Holly who was getting further and further away from me. Jed stood beside her. I could see "Don't be mad at me!" written all over her face, while mine must have read "I'll never forgive you."

"So, how did you like my story?"

"What story?"

Yeah, good strategy, I'll play dumb like someone who wasn't discovered hiding in the closet last night with torn out pages from your book.

"You know those two pages that were mysteriously torn out of my book."

"Why would I have torn out any pages of *your book*, if I had the chance to read the whole thing?"

"Well, I'd very much like to know that myself."

*Wipe that stupid grin off your face, man!* Okay, he might have won this time, but I'm not going to let him know.

"Does she know?" I asked him, pretending that I was interested in his love life with someone else.

"I guess so."

If he insists on discussing his feelings for Cassie, well, so be it.

"Well, Little Miss Cassie has a boyfriend, so it seems that you've messed this one up, dear Adam."

We sat in an awkward silence until we reached the top of the hill. Before we got out, Adam turned to me and asked in a less friendly voice.

"Really, that's all you have to say about it?"

"What did you expect? That I'd be overjoyed because you're in love with someone else?"

"What the hell are you talking about?"

"What the hell am I talking about? What the hell are you talking about? And anyway, how dare you take that tone with me?"

"I'll speak however I want to, especially when I'm telling you that you are one crazy woman! Have you read my book at all? You must have only read a half a page, because if you had read it, you'd know how much the book is about you. Anyway, while we're at it, we might as well talk about Oliver."

We heard Miss Esther's voice, just in time. I didn't want to argue with someone who walks in and out of people's lives and who's convinced that that kind of behavior is alright.

"Hey, children and not children! Line up in pairs. You'll go down the slope one by one in a nice orderly manner. I'd like to ask the helpers to pay good attention to the safety of the youngsters.

*This day can't get any worse!* I've already fought with Adam and now I have to go down this terrifying slope in front of him, while he knows all too well, that I suck at this!

Holly sneaked up next to me and asked if I was okay.

"No, Holly, nothing is okay! Adam is crazy, you know I can't ski! I just want to go home, right now."

"Chill, girl! Tell me what happened!"

Holly made big eyes at me, as if it was a surprise to her that Adam was an idiot.

"The book is about me, isn't it? He's in love with someone, then he dumps me and that's the end of the story. Adam is a mad, crazy, insane, deranged, unhinged, psychopath screwball!"

My stomach shrunk into a tiny knot. Holly asked me to go first so she could be behind me and help me avoid embarrassing accidents.

That's what's going to happen, sure thing. I'll survive this just as I've survived everything else. I shouldn't think of the worst. Why couldn't I do it?

I assumed the position and I took off even before Miss Esther gave the sign. I was furious: why did everything need to be so complicated? Why can't my life be as simple as other people's?

I managed to get down the slope pretty easily until I remembered that I didn't actually know how to do any of this stuff. There was no break or trick to help me slow down. Well maybe there was, but I didn't know about it. If I remembered any of what Adam babbled about widening some part of my body like the shape of a *V* or something. Instead of the *V* I managed to fall so spectacularly that everyone stared at me. Well, I guess they were entertained because my head landed in a pile of snow. Judging from their laughter, my guess must have been correct.

"Are you okay?" Adam offered his hand, trying to hide his grin.

I, however, couldn't hide my feelings anymore.

"You want to talk about Oliver, right? Do you remember that you left? You left, you walked out and I waited for you in vain. You didn't come back. And do you know what hurts the most? That I couldn't stay angry with you. I waited for you no matter how long it took for you to decide to come back. Adam, for heaven's sake, I was in love with you! You can't break someone's heart, then come back as if nothing ever happened."

"Only in one case."

"What case could give anyone the right to walk back into my life so shamelessly?"

"If the boy is just as much in love with the girl."

I was fed up with him and the fact that he believed he could do and say anything he wanted to. Instinctually I slapped him, but he caught my hand. I jumped up from the snow angrily and wiped the snow from my clothes. I shot some furious glances in his direction just to make sure he felt that he was in the wrong.

I exploded into my room and fished out the crumpled pages from the bottom of my bag. Let's see that last page which bore the page number three:

"It started out as a usual Saturday night. The only difference was that I was planning to get wasted not with my friends, but all alone. My whole life had been pointless and if it had gone on like this, it would have made me sick. That's why I came back. I was fed up with girls coming and going in my life. I had nobody constant in my life except for my father. The reason was very simple, I didn't want anybody. I didn't want to have anybody in my life for long term. I didn't want to feel, I didn't want to give them the chance to abandon me like she did. My mother left when I was young, on my fifth birthday to be exact. She went off with another man. Dad tried to convince me that she would come back soon and we would redo my birthday party, but that was the least of my problems. After one month I had to accept that my mother would never ever come back. I hated every woman after that and the fact that someone could break my heart so much. I started to change. I became the one who inflicted the pain and not the one who was hurt. I didn't do it on purpose, I just didn't care. I could say that I was enjoying it, but the problem was that I didn't feel anything.

Our story started in a bar long before she'd suspected it. Her long, dark blonde hair softly, cascaded over her shoulders. She was shorter than me, leaning against the bar, checking out every guy that passed by.

It was written on her face that she had seen at least a thousand romance movies and came here every weekend just to find "the One" who probably only existed in her imagination. There was something about her that spoke to me, I wanted to catch her. I liked the idea that I could be someone's Prince Charming for an evening. Of course, she wasn't an uncomplicated girl, but what did I know at that point.

I went up to her with the usual "Can I invite you for a drink?" but she rejected it very quickly. I clearly remember her first sentence to me:

"Do you really think I'd really fall for your lame pick-up line and then turn away so you could slip something in my drink? Try that with her, over there, maybe she'll fall for it," she gestured towards the forty year old woman who was clearly thirsty for male company."

I'd never met a girl who made me laugh even for a moment. Usually my pick-up lines work, the bartender poured the drink into the girl's glass and I poured honeyed words from my mouth. The woman next to us would have probably been into me, but I didn't care. I didn't want to leave this girl, although clearly I wasn't her type. I asked her if she didn't want to drink with a stranger, why was she here. She answered, again full of sarcasm, that it surely was not because of me. I had strange feelings about her. It annoyed me that she was so full of herself, she drove me crazy and it bugged me just as much as it intrigued me. Not because it was a challenge but because this made her different from all the other girls. She was the complete opposite of all the girls I'd met before. Her friends came back and she left without saying goodbye.

I spent the rest of the evening looking for a girl like her. Not her, but someone similar. Everyone can be replaced, I was sure to find a good enough copy. I found a similar girl not much later, who would have been up for an evening which started with a drink and ended in bed, but after the first glass I stood up and said goodbye to her. I didn't want the same thing I'd experienced a thousand times before, but something new. I headed home, but I found the Girl in the parking lot bothered by some chump. I went up to them and asked if everything was alright. The guy tried to show off, so I had to punch him. I'd learnt how to fight, but not how to feel. I didn't even know her name, but I was unable to walk on without her."

*Adam met me that night.* I was the one who sent him away and drove him crazy. Was he really writing about me? Was Cassie actually the annoying girl? I couldn't agree more, but he still couldn't do this to me. He'd already walked away once, so he didn't have any right to do any of this.

I thought about his book for the rest of the evening. I was conflicted because he didn't have the right to do this to me and

I didn't have the right to do it to Oliver. I imagined at least a hundred thousand versions of what I could do and I still felt incredibly stupid in this situation. My crazy heart always messed things up. It never let me make a clear-minded decision.

Holly was the only one who knew about this ordeal. Tracy was too immersed in her eye-games with Garrett and I was doing my best to avoid Adam. The easiest way to do that, was to play sick, that way I could stay in the hotel all day long.

Apparently, Adam tried to see me at least six time, but my faithful bodyguard did a good job in keeping him away. Holly saw through my fake "illness" right from the start, but she told Adam that it was contagious. If we want to be honest, I was actually suffering from something contagious, and it was Adam who'd infected me. We could certainly say it's all his fault.

I felt like I had lived in a false world up until then because I was unable to accept that in reality I could be abandoned at any moment, even if I felt like everything was perfect. Then he returned as if nothing had happened, he opened my eyes and I realized that I had made the wrong choice. I made a mistake and I wanted to correct it, even if that meant making another mistake or hurting someone else. I wasn't the one who walked away, so why did I feel so horrible?

There was a knock on the door, but Holly wasn't looking after me anymore because she'd gone hiking with the others. I wasn't ready to talk to him. I hadn't managed to talk to Oliver either, although he called me a million times. I needed to gain time, but how?

*I'll pretend not to be here.* Of course this has been my stupidest idea so far because if he is knocking, he must be aware that I was in and he's determined to talk to me. *I'll pretend to be sleeping. I'll tell everyone that I'm sleeping, so I can't hear anything.* It's normal, when someone's sick they sleep all day and I am very sick. I tried to lie motionless and pretend to be fast asleep.

"Amy, I know you're in there, I can hear your TV. Please let me in, we have to talk."

I am not going to become a spy that's for sure, remaining unnoticed is not my forte. However, the voice behind the door reassured me because it wasn't Adam's but Trevor's.

I jumped up and opened the door.

"Sorry to bother you, I just want a few minutes from your life, if it's not a problem. Holly told me that you were sick and indeed you don't look too well, so if you want, I can come back later."

I don't look so well? I'm not even sick.

"Don't worry, we can talk for a minute. Thanks for the

compliment, you really want to tell me that I look like shit?"

"You know that's not what I meant."

"What do you want to talk about?"

"There is a one-year internship opportunity which could help you a lot with your future career. My niece reads your articles regularly and she was the one who told me about you. The management has had their eye on you for a while so now they've chosen you. After the one year's passed, you'll have the opportunity to work with a more famous magazines. You don't have to answer right away, just give it some thought."

That's what I've been dreaming about since I was small, and now I feel like it couldn't be more easy. Usually if good things happen to us, we have to give up some other things.

"This sounds great, but there must be a catch."

"Yeah, there is a tiny drawback, you're right. You'd have to finish school as a correspondence student, but I've already discussed this with Miss Esther. There's something else: it's in a different state. So you'd need to say goodbye to your life here."

I couldn't speak. I'd never been so far away, especially not for so long. Not to mention the fact that at the moment, my life's a disaster and I'm nowhere near the top of my game. However, this has been my childhood dream and now I have the chance to make it come true. If I don't take this chance, I'll regret it for the rest of my life, even if that means I have to let go of love. What love? The one who already let go of me?

"I'd lie if I said that it hasn't been my childhood dream, but at the moment my life is pretty messed up, so I don't know if I can just walk out on everything and everyone, just like that."

"Amy, please just think about it! It's about your future. This is one of those "chance of a lifetime" opportunities that everybody mourns if they don't take it."

"You know, I'm still at a loss for words that you've even considered me for the position. How much time do I have to decide?"

"A week. The course starts next week."

One week? That means I'd just have time to go home, pack my things, say goodbye to my family and leave. Trevor left me in a similar way and I went ballistic.

I can't leave, not now! This is not my moment. Or could it actually be my moment?

I wanted to call Ruby to ask for advice. While I waited for Holly to come back or for me to have enough strength to call Ruby, I figured out my basic problem: I always waited for someone else to make a decision for me, to give me the answer, to show me the correct way. I blamed Adam for everything when I was the one who had never confessed my feelings for him, I just expected him to figure it out from my behavior. It was a bit problematic because my actions toward him suggested that he annoyed me. I always expected others to solve my problems for me, but this time it had to be me. I had to make this decision alone, otherwise I would never grow up. However, I had to admit that I didn't really know what I wanted. I hadn't found my place anywhere. I wanted everything to change but I wanted someone else to make the decision to change things for me because I was unable to do so.

Everyone else got back in the evening. We had one day left on the trip and I had spent the majority of my time hiding from Adam. Oliver texted me, we need to speak right away. I couldn't put off talking to him, any longer. I could say I felt horrible, but it wouldn't be the truth. I got what I deserved. Oliver told me that he'd made a mistake. He went to a party and that girl was there. The one he told me so much about the evening we met. Yea, the ex-girlfriend. Karma is a funny thing, isn't it? The girl was there and I was here and not with him. He didn't know what had got into him, but things happened and he felt horrible and he was terribly sorry and he didn't want to lose me. I could have told him that I couldn't forgive him and we should forget each other, ease my own sense of guilt, but I was unable to. Instead I decided to tell him everything, from the beginning. We talked for almost two hours. I didn't want to hang up because I knew that once our conversation was over, so was our relationship. He wasn't Adam, he was the closest thing to him. People often believe that when a relationship is over you can still be friends, even if you need a little time. The truth is, however, that if the relationship is over, your friendship is never going to be the same. I hung up and started to cry. I sat outside at the wooden tables and I watched the falling snow. I hated being in love with Adam. I was cold and I wanted to head inside, but my legs didn't obey me. It was nice to sit outside and not think of anything. We had one day left, more exactly, one evening. My frozen arms suddenly felt warm, it was a huge blanket Adam snuggled around my neck.

"If you insist on freezing outside and getting even sicker, you will need this, don't you agree?"

What could I say? The only thing I needed and my only remedy was you.

"Yes, thank you!"

"Are you alright?" He gave me a look I'd never seen before.

This could be the moment when I confess everything to him, even the things I'd just managed to admit to myself. I still loved him and it was not going to change.

"Sure."

*... in that minute, the sentences wouldn't come to me. When I sat next to him in silence and without enough courage to tell him that nothing's been alright in my life, since he left.*

"Amy, nothing is alright."

"Why?" I looked at him wide eyed and full of hope. I was hopeful that he'd say something that could make our complicated relationship unambiguous.

"Because I owe you this." He approached me slowly, leaving me the chance to jump up and escape if I wanted to. I didn't want to. I didn't want anything else, but for him to kiss me and our relationship to start up again.

"What do you owe me?" I gave him a curious look as if I had been interested in something more than his kiss.

"You know, the mistletoe."

He pulled me closer and kissed me. We spent the last night of the trip together. The next day we packed our bags together and he sat next to me on the bus. I felt like we were in kindergarten. I think Holly, Tracy and the whole group knew the news already. It would've been difficult to not notice because my joy was written all over my face. Holly offered Adam the chair next to me even though she wanted to travel beside me to gossip. Garrett and Tracy got far enough in their "relationship" to exchanged numbers. I know, I know you're curious about what happened to Holly and Jed?

Well, that remains a question for them to figure out. Holly announced that she'd break up with her boyfriend because they had no future together. Jed could only hope she would. Adam and I spent the whole evening and the whole ride home together, talking. It was good to look at him, to sit next to him, to be with him and finally feel happy. On the way home, I rested my head on his shoulder; I wasn't afraid of him leaving me anymore, actually I'd never been this sure of myself. For once, I was the one who decided for something else.

Once we got home, I sat down to talk with my parents. I told them everything. Mom didn't say anything, neither did dad. They told me that whatever I decided, they would support me. I'd never felt like I knew what I wanted do with myself for the rest of my life. I'd always chased after love and now I had it. But life couldn't be only about that. Not until I'd figured out what I wanted to achieve. I accepted the internship Trevor offered and thus, I made my own decision. If I wasn't able to find happiness alone, I'd never be happy with someone else. I packed my luggage and said my goodbyes. I couldn't bring myself to tell anyone that I was leaving except for Ruby. I couldn't leave her without a word. I invited her over in the evening and she jumped all over me, she was so happy that Adam and I were finally an item.

After I told her about the sad turn of events, she started to cry and smash things. She told me that if I was on the run because of Adam, she'd kill him.

She'd push him under a bus if it makes me stay. But it wasn't about Adam, it was about me, my life, and the direction I was headed. I didn't know where I was going but at least I knew I had to figure it out, alone. Ruby didn't know how to stop crying and she even threw out my carefully packed things from the suitcase in attempt to make me stay. She didn't give up until after the third time.

"If you really want to leave, I'll let you go. But one year is a really long time. You've never been so far from me, for so long and you can't be. Amy, nothing will be the same without you."

"Ruby, I'm going to come back. I'm not leaving forever. And you know our friendship is for life."

She hugged me and left with tears in her eyes.

I didn't say goodbye to Adam, I just wrote him a letter that Ruby delivered. I asked her to only give it to him the next day, so that he wouldn't have a chance to stop me. The strange thing was that for the first time, I didn't spend the whole night debating if I'd made the right decision or not.

I didn't even regret it. *I had to leave, I simply had to.*

The taxi driver rang in the morning, at seven sharp.

Adam was afraid, he was a coward, he left, but he loved me. I ran into the arms of Oliver from my emotions. I made mistakes, we made mistakes, maybe I made bigger ones because I lied to other people, my friends and even to myself. Everybody knows, me included, that Adam was the right one for me. If a girl on the verge of adulthood can use big words like that. I know it's him. It's simple as that. You just look at him and you know. You know that he makes your world tremble and that's the end of it. You're not looking for someone else, you don't want anybody else, but him. If he leaves, you'll wait for him because you know you belong together. And you know he'll return because it's your destiny. He finds his way back to you and you're willing to close your eyes to the time and years you lost, it's as if he stepped into my life just the day before. Maybe you even managed to let him go, but everything changes when he comes back because everything begins again. You and him, a never-ending story.

I said goodbye to my parents and to the old Amy and I got in the car. On the way to the airport I kept thinking about what Adam would do once he got my letter. Honestly, I didn't know if I was going to regret my decision, I didn't even know if I was doing the right thing. Actually, the closer I got to the airport, the more convinced I became that I was going to mess everything up. However, the feeling grew in me that my current decision would be the biggest mistake in my life only if I wasn't willing to make it again. If I had to choose again, I would definitely decide to set out by myself on a journey to find myself.

# Chapter Eleven

"I must be crazy, but I think you have just said…"

"No, you heard it correctly. I've avoided these words all my life, but now I've said them. I love you and I want to spend the rest of my life with you."

The years might have deepened my friendship with Holly, but my first phone call was still going out to Ruby. I was so excited, I imagined a thousand different ways of how I could tell Ruby.

It's ringing and ringing and ringing.

"Yes?"

The phone almost fell out of my hand but I tried to get it back despite the shock.

It was his voice.

Love, this freaking thing. If I say yes, I'll lose part of my life, the part which still thinks that Adam is the One, if I say no then the part who thinks it is Shon. The question is, who do I love more: him or myself?

Years went by, but it was as if it all happened yesterday. I really walked out of his life five years ago - I was so confident. I took the big world in my arms, I left everything behind, him included, and yet I still felt like a silly teen girl when I've heard his voice.

I was watching the phone on the floor, but I didn't have enough strength to pick it up. Why would I have? It was just Adam on the other side, nobody important, just a boy from my past.

Come on, Amy, it's the boy you had a crush on so many years ago. Now, years later, you still drop the phone when you hear his voice.

It's a strange feeling knowing that no matter how much time might have flown by us, we can still tremble and fall all over again because of someone's voice. I do believe in signs, in things bigger than us, but it can't be a sign. This must just be a bloody coincidence: at the exact moment I'm proposed to, he suddenly, mysteriously reappears, really?

How many times will I have to write him out of my story to prevent him from getting a new chapter? He had enough of it already, wasn't it enough? Why does he want to be the protagonist when he's not such a big deal?

Oh, yes he does, says my childhood self to contradict my adult self.

Where should I begin the rest of my story? Maybe I'll start with the moment I left.

# Five years ago

In the airport I had about fifteen minutes to change my mind and rewrite our story, but I didn't do it. Part of me wanted Adam to appear, another part, maybe the stronger side, wanted it to be over.

I stood there, clutching a magazine in my hand and all I could think about was that, it all had to be exactly this way. How else could it be? I had ten minutes left before the boarding, when I saw a familiar suitcase being pulled next to me.

"On a scale of one to ten, how excited are you?"

I lifted my head and…

I know, everyone wants to know if Adam had followed me? Did he manage to stop my plane before it took off? Well, the answer is no. He didn't run after me, we didn't fall into each other's eyes. He let me go, he let me board that freaking plane and find what I'd set out to find. So I guess films and their big stories about love aren't true after all.

Lifting my melancholic gaze, I noticed Holly standing there. She didn't care about the hundreds of other people waiting around us, she started shouting:

"I'm coming with you!"

I didn't care about the details, I was just so happy to see her. Last year they'd offered the opportunity to Holly but she chose love and stayed. One year later, she'd matured enough to choose for herself and since the other student backed out, Holly was able to come with me. Later I found out the other student, the one who chose not to come, was Ruby.

We talked the whole flight, to the big pleasure of the

people sitting around us. There were so many things racing through my head that I wanted to tell Holly, but I felt like I didn't need to say anything, because she understood exactly what was going on inside me.

It's difficult to give up your life and choose the great unknown instead. There is only one thing that could be even more difficult: to give up on a life and place, where your prince charming had found you, where everything was like in the fairy tales, until that point when you pack your suitcase because you've realized that there's more to life than this, because you believed that you could really change the world even if you're just a silly little girl. Yeah, I'll speak more about changing the world later.

Let's start with what happened right after our arrival. When our plane landed successfully, Trevor gathered the team. She introduced us to two friendly-looking girls: Dana and Laine and mentioned a third girl, who reminded me of Cassie and was very antipathic. She announced she would arrive on a later plane, but nobody really listened to her because we were busy with the excitement of arriving to a new city with our new question; where would we spend the night.

Trevor was such a great organizer that he'd expected us one week later. The result was that we spent our first week in a rundown motel. We couldn't complain because what did we risk? Worst case scenario we would've been massacred and kidnapped, or devoured by cockroaches. Seriously, we couldn't have got in any serious trouble even if we'd wanted to.

After we arranged our things in the motel, Trevor asked me to go back to the airport with him. His secrecy started to bug me, I didn't understand why I needed to go with him.

"Amy, I guess you don't have any idea why I asked you to come with me. I'm aware that you're not the best of friends and that the past few weeks had made the situation even worse, but I'd like to ask you to be the more mature one. We are almost adults, with mistakes, yes but we're not in kindergarten anymore."

Trevor kept talking, but I had no idea what he was blabbering about. I couldn't imagine that there could possibly be a worse surprise than him announcing Adam, just to add a newer phase to our endless orbiting of each other.

I liked the new city, the roads, the buildings and people seemed somehow happier. All in all, I liked it here until...

We got out of the taxi and saw Trevor's surprise guest. Their plane landed earlier, so she waited for us, sitting on her suitcase. Suddenly, I didn't like the streets and the trees anymore, not to mention the people. Well, specifically I didn't like the one person who crouched opposite us on the airport.

Cassie.

Speaking of the devil, if it had been any other girl sitting there alone, I'm sure that somebody would've tried to hook up with her or kidnap her, but it was Cassie. Nobody wanted her. I think if someone kidnapped her, they would send her back three days later with priority postage.

*Who hates me enough that to send this blood-sucker after me? Who and Why? Oh, I know! This was my punishment for not being content with my happiness, that destiny had already offered me and as a punishment, I was given Cassie. But it's okay because as Trevor had put it: we're mature adults. At least I was, I wasn't that sure about Cassie.* I'll just go on pretending that she doesn't exist, which was a bit complicated in her case because being a blood-sucker, she's always where she is not welcome and she always knows about everything she shouldn't know about.

Apparently Cassie had packed her whole flat, so Trevor asked me to help her load it into the trunk.

Of course, why wouldn't I help? It's been just a year since this dimwit kissed the boy... I've just abandoned?

While I tried my best to list my reasons for hating Cassie, I accidentally dropped one of her expensive bags on the floor. I barely managed to not kick her bag before quickly grabbing it. I got in next to Cassie towards the back, while Trevor sat in the front. I didn't care about the new environment or the work anymore, I ignored Trevor's failing efforts to try to lighten the mood with funny stories. Especially after he'd told me that Cassie and I would be roommates. I wanted to start a new life. It was going to be difficult to start a new life, if I was going to spend the first magical period of my new life with someone I hated from the bottom of my heart, so much so that her voice made my hair grow on my legs. Just the sight of her, made me want to throw up my lunch.

Getting back to the others, Holly immediately saw that there was a problem. A few seconds later the problem got out of the taxi.

"Is this a joke?"

"I wish it was!" I answered with a sour face.


In those first weeks, we were introduced to our new jobs. Our task was to collect, correct and write articles. Every week we were given a new topic we needed to dissect. We also had our personal projects and the best one was published in the "Discover new talents" column of the magazine.

I fell even more in love with writing and everything around it. Of course this new found love didn't make me forget the old one, but it filled my life. I thought a lot about my parents, my dog, Ruby and yes, Him.

I knew that Ruby hated me and that she would never forgive me for leaving, even though she also had the chance to do the same. My only consolation prize, was that I knew that she was loved. She'd found happiness alongside Aaron and it was enough for me.

She tried to seduce me into to coming back home with all sorts of different reasons, but I never gave in. I didn't even reach for my suitcase when she went as far as to lie that Ian Somerhalder, was in our town. No, I didn't pack my suitcase like a crazy little girl would and rush over there to see him.

Each time we talked on the phone Ruby hinted at the fact that her life would be much easier if she didn't miss me so much. I was upset with her because she could've come with me. And somewhere deep down I was also jealous of her.

We had a dream when we were little. We believed that we would change the world together. As we grew older this dream world grew smaller. I had to be strong in my new life, but in the beginning not a day went by, that I didn't miss Ruby, my parents and Him like hell. I missed my old life and many times I felt like giving up this new one just to go back to where I had been.

I promised myself that I wouldn't try to find out what Adam was doing since I was the one who left him. However, there came a period when I missed him so much that I started investigating. Any girl in love knows exactly how I felt. He wasn't my friend on social media, but that didn't prevent me from investigating his profile every day. One night, however I didn't see his usual grinning face, instead I saw something totally different. The glass I was holding fell out of my hand and shattered into pieces on the floor, alerting the others that something was awfully wrong.

Adam was in a relationship. Slowly, I pieced the picture of him and his new girl, together. Adam was in a relationship with a brown-haired ugly toad. Adam had moved on, as if that was even possible. In reality, Adam was travelling around with his new girl. Adam was travelling with someone who wasn't me. My heart missed a beat. I should have been the one he was travelling with. He should have selfies with me, he should be in a relationship with me. He'd struggled with me for six months and nothing happened and now this Miss Nobody wormed her way into the social media life of my Adam.

Me, who was honest with him, opened her heart to him, bared her soul to him, was never good enough to parade around in public, but this hag was!

Any girl in love would also know that there's no real logic in any of our deeds and the fact that I left him didn't mean that I didn't love him! Quite the contrary!

After one year away from home, Holly had enough of my pitiful situation. When I finally understood that Adam was over me, a new era started. Even though I'd already started a new life, it still felt like my old one with the tiny exception that our paths had diverged.

Back home, Tracy and Ruth became best friends and Ruth

gave put up a fight for Jed, a fight where in she was the only fighting because Jed's little heart beat only for Holly.

As for Jed... there wasn't a month, week, day, minute or second that he wasn't trying to get in touch with Holly. We were of course very happy about that, especially when he thought the best time to share his measly feelings with Holly was at three in the morning. Completely wasted at the time of his nocturnal confession, he thought it would be a good idea to repeat the wondrous news to her again, at seven in the morning.

Holly loved Jed no matter how much she tried to hide it from us. Love cannot be hidden. When someone's in love, you can see it on their face, their smile, their behaviour, their interaction with others. You can find it in their words, in their sentences.

I didn't realize how serious Holly's feelings were until we went home for Christmas. Our old friends organized a party and invited everyone. The party was raging when Holly burst into the room with teary eyes howling:

"Where is Jed?"

I searched, but couldn't answer her because I hadn't seen Jed all evening. Holly told me through fits of crying that a car that looked just like Jed's had an accident and she couldn't get in touch with him. My whole body trembled when I heard her words. In the end, we managed to get a hold of Jed's friend and sadly confirmed that they indeed had an accident.

In a matter of seconds, we were on our way to the hospital. Holly kept blaming herself for the accident, during the whole ride over.

"It's all my fault, how could I be such an idiot? I love him, why the hell was I playing games? You know these games are stupid, if you're playing, you're taking away your own chance, you know what I mean? You're taking away you chance to be happy. Dear God, how could I have been such an idiot?"

I tried to calm Holly down and convince her that nothing that bad could've happened, not to them. When we got to the hospital, the doctor reassured Holly and Jed's family that Jed was going to be alright and that he was going to get away with just a broken leg, and even that wasn't the worst.

I had to go outside, I couldn't stand hospitals. I watched the fog and secretly hoped that He, would somehow magically step out of it. Maybe he would appear and … I don't know what I expected. All knew for sure was that, I wanted to see him. I wanted him to appear and tell me that everything was going to be okay. Not just in the world, but with us too. I was the one who left, I should have been the one to go after him, but I still waited for him to come back for me even though it wasn't his responsibility because this time, he wasn't the one who left me. My own decision was driving me mad.

Holly wanted to stop her scholarship but Jed dissuaded her. In the end, I finally understood why she chose love over her career, a year before. I thought I'd really messed everything up. What if something happens to Adam while I'm gone? What if we'd never be able to tell each other how we really felt? Why? Because we chose to play stupid games with each other that never made any real sense. Life will just pass us by without us ever having had the chance to enjoy it.

# Chapter Twelve

After the accident, Holly dared to confess her love to Jed. Not in secret, not hiding it from herself, but in a way that Jed could know it too.

I managed to run into Oliver at that tragic Christmas party, but we didn't have much to say to each other, even though I missed him. I would've had lots of things to tell him, but we just walked past each other like two strangers who'd never laughed together, never cried during their last phone call, so like two people who'd never gone out together.

Did I run into Adam on that trip? No.

When I went home, Ruby told me, without me having to ask, that he wasn't here. He was gone. Her tone of voice was as if he'd been a fugitive. My past year was all about him even though we had nothing whatsoever to do with each other. On the positive side, Jed managed to convince her that it would be a stupid idea to give up on her dreams, so once he got out of the hospital, he'd be moving in with us.

As I went around in town, I noticed unhappiness on people, I spent my time watching people.

Where are they rushing to, so fast? Where was I rushing off to?

An odd feeling ate itself into my brain and I suddenly felt that you could actually miss out on love, by arriving too late.

Whatever I had said or thought earlier, I still believed that he'd come after me, that he'd stop me and that there'd finally be no more questions in my head. I'd managed to repress this feeling, I lied to myself, saying that it was all meant to be this way, but for heaven's sake! Why would it need to be like this?

Because I wanted it this way? No, I didn't want it this way. I'm a woman and I'm an idiot, but he knew it. He knew it when he fell for me.

My life hadn't really changed, at all. I don't know what I was thinking. Everything's so easy in the movies. One character leaves home and new love knocks on their door the next day. There's no suffering for years, or things like the love you left, finding someone new before you do. But we shouldn't just focus on my mistakes.

By the way, about mistakes and films. Why didn't he come after me? Who cares what I wrote to him in my letter? In the movies the boy always plucks up his courage and conquers the girl, so that's how you get the happy ending and not just *The End*. The male protagonist isn't supposed to stay home, counting his blessings letting the girl he loves fly away to a different universe. Why couldn't Adam stay in his role as my knight in shining armor?

Don't I know why? Because destiny intended someone else for him, not me. Even if I would've been the perfect girl for him. Well, destiny had other plans: the brown haired, not at all pretty, old-fashioned Juliet. Even though I was supposed to play that role, with my cool hair and all my other cool things.

I saw tiny thought-bubbles above my head with Adam demanding I take his hand and ride off into the sunset with him. I place my hand in his, hold on tight and we ride our unicorn into infinity and beyond.

Our new life had a lot of other surprises for us: new friends, new enemies and new mistakes. By mistakes I mean, the jerks who forgot to call me after dates, even though I thought we had a great time. Maybe we shouldn't disregard the fact that during the majority of my dates I talked about Adam, making it very clear that I was no longer interested in him. From the rate of my successful dates, I might not have been too convincing.

After Jed moved in with us, I started to feel completely alone. Jed asked thousands of touchy questions even though

Holly always poked him when he did.

"Why did you let Adam go without a word?"

Of course, it was all my fault! What about the time, he left me. Was that okay? Of course it was, because you're boys and you can pull off shit like that. You can break girls hearts without being jerks, but if we do such a thing, you call us all kind of names. Typical.

"It was meant to be this way," I answered, sounding more or less convinced, while I crossed my fingers behind my back.

"Maybe so, but I just hope you know that he really loved you."

Of course, so much so, that he didn't chase after me at the airport.

On that fateful Saturday night Holly and I decided to go partying, we invited our cool colleagues. The only two that were cool: Dana and Laine.

Dana was full of energy, while Laine was the "I'll go out once a year to see what's happening in the world" type. Holly wanted to invite Cassie too because unlike me, she managed to make peace with her during the course of the year.

Of course, she wasn't the one who'd been humiliated by that snake, in front of the love of her life.

We let Dana choose the place. As expected, she managed to find the most popular club in town, which lined up all the biggest jerks of the city. Most of the men, well I find the word "men" a gross exaggeration for them, wore shirts and jeans. If you walked through the crowd, you noticed that almost every guy looked exactly the same. Holly told Jed very clearly that he should dress up nice, which led to him appearing in a shirt-jeans combo. I didn't dare laugh openly, Laine and Cassie did it for me. I don't think Cassie had the right to laugh at Jed or to even breathe around us, because we weren't good friends. I just stood in the queue, looking for excuses to call it an early night. Noticing my expression, however, Dana announced that we were all going to leave together.

I wasn't a big drinker, I think the last time I actually

touched alcohol was that night when I met Adam. However, if I wanted to survive this night, I'd have to drink a lot, at least that's what I was able to judge from looking at the people around me. While Holly told Jed off, the others and I sneaked off to the bar. Cassie poked me and gestured towards the entrance.

"Hey, that guy has been staring at you since we came in."

I glanced in his direction and indeed a bearded guy was staring at me, intensely. I told Dana not to look at him so openly because he might come up to us.

I'd decided to change my life, besides having exiled myself to a different state, I decided to change my mind as well. If in the past I said no, in the present, now, I proudly proclaim, Yes (except of course, when it comes to drugs or any other mind altering substances or that annoying question, do I still love Adam and if I'd take the trash out), if someone paid me a compliment, I'd say thank you, like an adult and I'd never run to Ruby to laugh about it, again.

That's how this evening started. I promised myself that I'd show a new Amy to the world. Anyway, that bearded jellyfish kept moving closer toward us, or rather to the bar. When he got close to us he bothered the bartender:

"A whiskey on the rocks, please!"

"How polite," I thought to myself. He turned his head to the side and looked at me. One of his hands was groping the bar.

The word that came to my mind was not as much "sexy" but "sexual criminal." I looked at the bartender and something miraculous happened. Cassie and Dana whispered in my ears that he was kinda cute. True enough, since my first thought when I looked at him wasn't to throw up, but something very different. This was the historical moment when I suddenly felt *that thing* again. I don't know exactly what or why or how, but when I looked into his eyes, the world seemed to stand still. If one could fall in love with a look, it was that look. It petrified me. In that moment I not only forgot Adam's name, but also my own.

"Sixteen bucks for a drink, does it have gold in it, or what?"

"Yep, I'd like to ask for sixteen crunchy dollars. Are you going to pay for it or are you going to keep wasting the ladies' time?" answered the boy, who seemed to be an embodiment of all my dreams, with a whiskey bottle.

Mr. Cheap stared at him, then asked me if he couldn't buy me a drink. The question held the answer already, especially after the scene he'd just made. Sure thing, he barely wanted to pay for his own drink, why would he pay for mine?

I promised that I'd changed: I'd say yes instead of no and I'd give everyone a chance. Everyone except… Oh, to hell with the whole thing! My big transformation can wait. I quickly left Mr. Cheap and followed my girls to the dance floor. My friends could barely hold their laughter, it was so typical that the only caveman in the party would find me, of all people.

It was pretty difficult to dance in this place because the girls danced by twisting their body and writhing in front of the guys standing at the bar, while the latter danced by nodding their heads and tapping their feet, not letting go of their drinks for one single minute.

Holly and Jed disappeared, so the four of us were left alone. The others didn't notice, but I was secretly exchanging looks with the bartender. The party was so lame, that even Dana was forced to admit defeat. She kept insisting that she knew another good place in the city, but since she was the one who brought us here, nobody trusted her new big idea. We were making our way to the cloakroom when someone grabbed my arm.

"You kept staring at me all night long and now you're just going to leave, like that?"

I couldn't speak. The bartender stood in front of me, grinning his magnificent smile at me. Again, one of those stupid feelings when you know you shouldn't say anything, but you still do I said:

"Shouldn't you be working?"

Did I really just say that? Did I seriously tell him that he should go back to work? Alright. I failed at picking up guys again. My only excuse was that I accompanied everything I said with my best smile.

"My shift finished exactly two minutes ago. So where are we going, now?"

I needed to make up for my previous sentence.

"We're actually going somewhere else because we find this party boring."

Boring? I don't think I was heading on the right road to correct my mistakes.

That's why nobody wanted me anymore, because all I ever did was bullshit all the time. Couldn't I just tell him that we'll go wherever he wanted to go? He just needed to look at my ogling eyes and he could have figured it out, anyway.

"Boring? I don't see what you mean. Do you find the boy-entrancing choreography of those girls boring?" he laughed. "I know a place you might like, though."

First rule: Don't talk to strangers. Second rule: If you do, don't follow them anywhere. Third rule: If the kind stranger has beautiful blue eyes, forget the first two rules, bid goodbye to your loved ones and let's go.

Who cares about the rules anyway, as long as I had my friends with me? *Yep, typical stupid girl mentality; nothing bad can happen to me as long as I'm with my herd.*

"Wait a sec! How do we know this isn't a clever trick? You make us go with you, we naively follow, then you lock us up and do terrible things to us."

"We're busted, Chester. Let's go!"

He laughed with his friend and took another step towards me.

The way he held his hands in his pocket was so familiar. He stood in front of me like Adam did. A long, long time ago.

"Don't you think, if I had ulterior motives like that, I would've put something in your drink? Like an hour ago. You watch too many crime procedurals, don't you?"

"Oh, now that you mention it, I feel quite dizzy. Yeah, I'm

definitely starting to pass out. Security!"

"You don't need the show, it's not a live screening. It'd be pretty bad if I needed to rely on those methods."

"Unless it's your plan to gain our trust then strike afterwards."

"Aren't you a little paranoid?"

He arched an eyebrow and gave me a wondering look.

"Don't you think I need my paranoia in this world?"

"Look, I've been working here for four years. You caught my fancy and I have no other plans than just taking you out for dinner, seducing you to my bed and maybe if you stop being cheeky, I'd even go out with you. That's all."

Everybody around me started to laugh and I stood there in silence. Dana poked me to shut up and let him come with us. Her sister knew all the bartenders here, so she knew there couldn't possibly be any problems.

"Okay, let's go."

I gave in, why not?

"By the way, let me introduce myself. I'm Shon and I like you."

"I'm Amy and I'm a bit paranoid."

"Dear Amy, since you have been so charmingly cautious, I have to admit that I like you too, but even more."

"Because I've talked so much B.S.?"

"No, because you have your wits about you."

We left the bar with Shon and his friend, Chester. They told us that there was a club a few blocks away, where they do great retro parties. They assured us that there would be fewer peacock-boys and wriggling girls.

Shon took my hand and we walked like that, while Chester tried to chat Cassie up, but she was visibly not up for it.

Shon told the security guards that we were with them and the guard let us in. This new place was completely different from the previous one. It was full of young people like us, there were no wriggling girls or empty-headed fashion magazine trolls.

Immediately, I liked the place and more importantly, I

liked Shon. I liked this city and I started to like my new life.

Dana and Cassie were on their third drink when Laine told us that she was feeling sick. Shon and I went out for some air, with her and after about fifteen minutes she felt better, so we went back in.

Shon kept holding my hand and I didn't want him to let it go. At any moment, the evening could've taken a turn and Shon and I fall head over heels in love with each other and become a happy couple... But of course, if had it happened that way, it wouldn't have been my story. I was used to the fact that with me, nothing's ever simple, especially not relationships.

Getting back to my girls, Cassie pulled me away from Shon and asked me to go with her to the restroom because something happened. However, we walked towards the exit and not the restrooms.

"Amy, we have to go home right now. I'm not feeling too well. I'm going to tell the others, please wait for me here."

"You should stay here and I'm going to find them. But what's wrong, are you okay?"

"No, Amy please, you should stay outside."

"What's happening, Cassie? What happened in the last fifteen minutes that I'm not aware of?"

"You don't want to know."

"Actually, now that you say that, I want to know even more."

"If I tell you, you're going to hate me even more than you already do."

"Have you kissed Shon?"

"What? No, but thanks for the suspicion."

"Why would I hate you? Come on, spit it out."

"It was as if I..."

"As if what?"

"As if I'd seen Adam."

One and a half years had gone by since I last saw him. They say that time solves every problem. Time makes you forget and brings you someone new. However, they tend to forget that there are cases when time doesn't. It could've been a week, a month or a year, when you meet Him again, time stands still. Time always takes you back to the moment of your beginning. Then two things can happen: the meeting feels you with a good feeling and you get lost in a whirlpool of time or you realize that your feelings for the others haven't change.

I was hit by the latter.

"Amy, please, let's go!"

"Why? It's okay. He and I? It's all in the past. Calm down, Cassie!"

"I know, but there is just one more thing."

"Spill it, what more can it be then my teen crush being here?" My voice grew thin from nervousness and I knew that Cassie was going to say something I wasn't ready for.

"He's here with his girlfriend."

I don't think you can ever be ready for this sentence. I pretended not to hear it because if I'd thought more about it, I'd have thrown myself under a bus. Even though, I was well aware that it was all my fault.

My legs trembled and couldn't decide what I wanted to do: to see him or to get away quickly like I'd done before.

One and a half years went by and I felt the same as if it had all happened yesterday. My thoughts drove me crazy and I started walking in circles in the club, looking for him. I wanted to see him although it was difficult to admit. I didn't care if he was alone or not because I was just looking for the moment. That moment when I'd see him again and he'd see me, and maybe he'd forgive me or maybe nothing would happen and I could move on because I got finally got closure.

Hunting for the moment, I circled three times and I ignored Cassie trying to grab to get me out of the club.

When I was just about to give up my search, I saw him standing at the entrance. There He was, the boy who made me cry so much I could've provided some desert countries with water. He stood there, leaning against the wall of the cloakroom, tapping his foot nervously. He crossed his arms.

159

However much I wanted to go to him I simply couldn't. I just stood there and watched. A few seconds later a brown-haired girl appeared and caressed his shoulder.

When you believe you're over it, that time has made you stronger, life swoops in to prove you wrong.

As an adult, I stood there feeling just like I did as a jealous teenager. Again, I was the seventeen year old Amy realizing that she was in love with Adam. The feeling hadn't change, but we had.

I have to get out. Immediately!

Turning around, I started slowly towards the exit. Fate had other plans for me. Fate took the shape of a tiny stall that I tumbled over. For heaven's sake, I didn't have time for this B.S.! I jumped up and hurried out of the club. Leaning against the wall outside, I tried to catch my breath, staring at the ground and I tried to forget what just happened.

I didn't really see him. He doesn't really mean anything to me. I don't really feel anything for him anymore. And I definitely didn't just see that hoe with him.

I couldn't decide what hurt more: to see him after all this time or to see him with someone else?

My tears started to fall. Couldn't stop rubbing my eyes and after each deep breath I repeated "I'm alright. I'm alright." When I managed to calm down, I saw a pair of black shoes in front of my eyes. I slowly lifted my head up and saw Adam looking back at me. I looked at him with teary eyes and I could only say one thing.

"I'm sorry."

Confusion filled his eyes and I saw he felt the same way I did. In that minute when we looked at each other, silently, a lot of things played out in my head. The feeling when he'd left me and I'd left him, the feeling I felt when Jed had an accident.

Maybe it was the latter that gave me strength to hug him. He hugged me with the same force I hugged him with. Finally, reciprocation. I didn't want him to leave his embrace, I didn't want the moment to end. He pushed my hair out of my eyes and hugged me even tighter.

"I'm happy to see you again," he whispered.

I didn't know what to tell him, I just stared straight ahead and I hated my younger self for leaving him. Maybe I just needed to grow up. Maybe I just needed more time because I was a child back then. Apparently, time had passed me by.

I never told him those sacred three words. Never, although I only truly felt them for him. I knew that life was so damned short and I didn't care what happened the next day. I didn't want to have regrets anymore when I thought about all the things I didn't do. Right then and there, I decided to say the words I secretly felt from the first, oh well maybe even the second or the third time we met.

"Adam, you don't have to say anything about what I'm going to tell you, but if I don't tell you, I'm going to hate myself for the rest of my life."

"Amy, you left. You left and you freaking didn't come back."

"I know and I was stupid. Please, don't be mad at me!"

"The years went by as well, don't you see? They passed us by and we can't do anything against it. We had a chance, actually if we want to be honest, we had a lot of chances and yet we didn't do anything. You're crying about the past, because you made a bad decision back then but I also made a bad decision for letting you go. I was such a coward for not chasing after you. But we have to grow up. We're too late, this feeling belongs to the past in our memories."

I didn't want to hear what he was saying. I stuttered, I could barely breathe.

"No, you're right. We both made mistakes, maybe I made bigger ones but when you say the word "late" my heart breaks."

"Why? You never reached out to me, you never came back, you never gave any sign of life to let me know you were okay. You know how I felt?"

"Yes, I know exactly."

"For heaven's sake, I didn't leave you for years, I only left for two measly months! I know I messed up, but I came back because I loved you! Tell me now, please, why your heart's breaking? Surely it's not because you were worried sick when you saw an accident on the local news. Would you like to know how many times I called Ruby at three in the morning begging her to talk to you, to ask you if you were alright? Exactly seventy times in six months. So, I'd like to know why your heart is breaking."

"Exactly because of this, because you loved me and I…"

"And you what?"

"Because I still love you the same way I always did."

He stared at me for about five minutes then he spoke in a trembling voice:

"Amy, it's over. You don't love me, you love *the thing* that we used to be."

Each of his words tore a piece out of me. It couldn't be over because I still loved him. Sadly, that was not enough. It was not enough because it was the first time that I ever felt like I didn't mean anything to him, I was just a memory. He didn't look at me the way he used to, so many times before. I didn't feel that tiny fire in him that still loved me. I felt only one thing: I screwed up big time!

He put his arm around me and I got the same kiss on the forehead as before. The only difference between the two kisses was that now I knew this one was for a good, as was his goodbye.

"Amy, I have to go."

I didn't look up from my falling tears because I saw that someone waited for him. I needed a little time to be able to lift my head and watch as he left with that other girl. I waited for him to turn around and come back to me, but he didn't.

# Chapter Thirteen

I didn't have any strength left to go back to the others, but I didn't need to. Cassie came for me a little while later. She didn't ask me anything, just put her arm around me. I couldn't stop crying and she didn't ask about anything. I hated Holly and Ruby because they weren't by my side. I hated the brown-haired girl who had stolen Adam from me. I hated Adam because he didn't love me anymore. I hated all the happy couples who left the club. I hated this place because if we hadn't come here, I would still be head over heels for the bartender. I hated myself for leaving him too.

Cassie took my hand and didn't let go.

"I know I've behaved quite stupidly in the past few years."

*Years? Let's call it your whole life.* Of course, I didn't say it out loud because I no longer felt that she was the one person on earth that I hated the most. Her place was now taken by that brown-haired bitch.

Cassie looked in my eyes as if she had read my thoughts. It was scary.

"Okay, so then I've just been an annoying pile of poop my whole life, is that any better? Hear me out, though. I know it sounds stupid, but you can count on me anytime, okay?"

At that moment I was unable to say anything. I couldn't think of anything other than the fact that Adam had really left me and that it was finally really, over.

It was a strange feeling when I put my arm around Cassie and… it was really nice. Even though she didn't ask me to forget about the past, I did. I'd also behaved stupidly with people on countless occasions and they still accepted me. I felt a little guilty because we'd gossiped and laughed about Cassie behind her back a gillion times and yet, she was the one who let me smear my melting foundation all over her jumper and she didn't even mention it.

*Will I ever be able to forget that she humiliated me in front of Dylan? No, no way.* I'm not going to ever forget that, but the bottom line was that we could start with a clean slate. I'd come here for a clean slate, and if I deserved it, so did she.

After I'd cried for half an hour, Cassie told me that she would get our stuff and I should wait for her outside. I wiped my tears and not much later Shon arrived.

"Are you alright?"

Sure. Except for my heart having been shattered, everything is peachy, dear Shon.

"I'll be alright."

I didn't know what to say. I could imagine what he must have thought of me. The night started perfectly, then Adam appeared, I abandoned Shon who didn't understand anything and now I lied to him -with tear-stained eyes- that everything was alright.

"Hope I'm not being too pushy, but who was this guy?"

"Someone who used to mean a lot to me."

"Used to?" He smiled shyly and hugged me.

His hug was nice, but I felt even more miserable now that everyone felt sorry for me.

"There's nothing wrong, don't worry. It's over. I needed closure. Now I really had it."

Shon laughed then gave me a mocking look.

"Okay, so will you come on a walk with me?"

If in the past I had said no, now I was going to say yes. Answering to the question if I loved Adam was no exception.

"Yes, gladly."


I knew from the very first moment I met him, that Shon was going to be just like the others. I liked the fact that he was going to trick me. It might sound silly, but in a way I wanted him to. Since Adam's goodbye broke everything in me, Shon couldn't have done any bigger damage in me, even if he'd wanted to. I was looking for danger, I was looking for someone who would touch me the same way Adam did and let's be honest, Shon proved perfect for that.

Cassie walked ahead with the others, Shon and I lagged behind. Everybody had already gone upstairs when we reached or house. We talked in the gate for hours, I didn't notice how late it was. It was late compared to what? Compared to seeing Adam after one and a half years and I still was able to flirt with another boy or compared to the fact that I needed to wake up at seven in the morning?

Shon told me about his job, his life and about his almost famous band. They sometimes played in local clubs.

Great! That's exactly what I needed. A musician!

Dad used to tell me when I was a child that I could date anyone except for musicians because he thought that all of them were scoundrels. He once elaborated on this, telling me that he also used to play here and there. I couldn't imagine my dad in the role of the heartbreaker, although apparently he only became serious after he met my mom.

Nothing happened between us that first night when I met Shon and let go of Adam other than me being reborn. Not even a kiss. Yes, not even a measly little kiss. Of course, it wasn't time for that, yet.

We exchanged numbers, but my phone didn't ring for days. I was too perfect for him too. No more problems. That was going to be my new attitude. Who cared about Shon and the other two hundred guys, who forgot to call me back?

I didn't. My voice wasn't trembling because that dim-wit forgot to call me back after our half-magical evening. I'm only saying bad things about him because it feels good to say them.

My girls tried to console me by saying that Shon must have lost my number. They stuck to that assumption, until I told them he'd walked me home, so even if he'd lost my phone number, he'd have my exact address.

Two weeks went by and I still had no news of him. I

completely gave up on him, until one evening while writing my articles I realized there's no such thing as perfect guys. All of them are full of faults. The ones you liked were surely crazy, so you had no chances with them unless you were crazy too. But if you're crazy and he's crazy, well then it's not going to be easy for you. I could say that I was crazy like Shon, but if I wrote crazy, it might've been offensive, if I wrote cool, it might've been too egotistic. So let's just say, we were a good match like the pea and its pod.

In the end, I came to the conclusion that either we accepted things as they were and we tried not to think too much about them, or we messed everything up, including the moment, the relationship and our chance to be happy, by overthinking it.

After my wise conclusions, I heard a knock on the door. When I opened it, I could barely believe my eyes.

"Surprise!"

Somebody cried. Somebody who'd been there for me my whole life. She jumped in my arms without asking and I couldn't imagine how I was able to live my life without her. You only feel like this when the person standing in front of you sees into your soul, as if they were your other half. Yes, it was Ruby.

We talked all evening long and did the same thing the next day and the day after that. I always had something to say when I was with Ruby, she was just that kind of person. Even if nothing special was happening in my life. I told her about Shon and Adam's dramatic appearance. Just like my other girls, Ruby also thought I'd freak out about Shon, after getting closure with Adam, since Shon didn't reach out to me, but honestly, I didn't care. I got to spend the whole week with my best friend! Only one boy could break my heart in this life and I was already over it and him.

Was I really over it, though?

To celebrate Ruby's arrival, we decided to go partying that weekend. A bit shy, I told Ruby that Cassie didn't belong to the dark side anymore, but ours. She was unable to accept it, but when I told her that Cassie was there for me when I fell to pieces after getting closure with Adam, she became more lenient with her. Ruby wanted to go to a retro party, so we went to the club where Shon took us a few weeks before. Dana, Laine, Holly, Cassie and us went out to paint the town red. The club's entrance was full of poster which advertised with gigantic letters:

The star guest of the evening is the famous Black Raven band. Starts at 11 pm.

The club was full of people. I managed to forget Shon until the moment we ran into him. Although I didn't want to notice him, my eyes fell on him and his new prey. Everyone thought I'd freak out, but nothing like that happened.

*Do I seem bothered? Why would it bother me that after Adam (and the others) he's the 670th guy who dumps me before we even got started? Would it piss me off? No way!*

Shon noticed us and was strangely confused. Fuelled by this, I caught the first boy who came my way and I started explaining him something. Poor guy, he had no idea what I was talking about, but it was okay, because I didn't either. He stood with his back to Shon so his expression didn't matter, which was lucky for me because anybody could see that he had no idea what was happening. I was just warming up in the conversation with the nice stranger when Shon stepped to us and whispered in my ear mockingly:

"Did you see last night's CSI episode? A guy just like that was the criminal of the week. Have you already done background research on him or do you want me to fetch his files?"

"You're very funny, but unlike you, he looks like a normal human being."

"Really? So should I get a change of underwear?"

Okay, so let me get this straight. He dumped me and now he's mocking me?

"Maybe for your new unlucky victim."

He looked at the girl waiting for him at the bar, then turned back to me. We had a verbal duel for five minutes, then I let it go. Shon had a victorious smile and was happy in the thought that he'd won. I didn't feel like wasting my time on him, so I went to look for my girls who'd disappeared in less than ten minutes.

My eyes were always on the lookout for Shon, even when I sat down next to Ruby. Naturally, the lamest guys came up to us, but since I saw that Shon was watching me I pretended to be available for new *human* relationships. My friends disappeared, again so I was left alone with a wet blanket guy.

I hadn't seen Shon for half an hour, so I wiped the forced smile off my face. While the nameless guy went to grab us a drink, I fished out my phone from the bottom of my bag. The music suddenly became quieter and I heard a familiar voice which strongly reminded me of the voice of the weatherman Lupert Mckenzy.

"We'll start in a few minutes and you can welcome the Black Raven on stage."


Dana ran back to our table a few minutes later.

"Amy, you're not going to believe this. Hold on tight."

I would hold on if I had someone to hold on to. If there was a Hulk around who would, well it'd be enough if he just called me back."

"Yeah, I'm holding on. Now what?"

*"Shon's band is playing tonight."*

"Good for him."

"Don't you want to see him?"

"Of course I do! So I'm heading home right now."

Why the heck would I want to see him? Dad was right. Musicians are all stupid. Shon is extra-extra-extra stupid. For letting such a great girl as myself get away. (I didn't find this in those self-help books, or did I?)

To be honest, I was really curious about the way he played music, the way he performed on stage, in one phrase; I was just really curious about him, in general. Shon was the lead singer and also played guitar. I listened to the concert, hiding in the back. I'd have never thought they'd play this well. I didn't understand what they were doing in such a tiny club. They were getting to the last song when Shon grabbed the mike and said.

"There's a girl here. A girl who's undoubtedly turned my head."

That's just my luck. I really like this guy and he's going to confess his love to some other girl who has cheap, home-made ombre hair.

"So there's this girl and I'd like to take the opportunity to tell her this: Dear very careful, CSI fanatic Amy! I'd like you to know that one day I'm going to marry you!"

Amy? What? Has he just said my name?

Dana grabbed my hand and lifted it up while shouting: It's her, it's her!

Ruby and the others all looked at me. In their eyes, I could see that very soon they'd burst out laughing. It didn't happen, though. Nobody laughed, they all smiled. They smiled at me in a very annoying way and I had no idea how to react because I'd never been in a situation like that. First, I needed to come to terms with the things Shon had just said, but my mind had gone blank after he said my name.

Shon and his band played their last song and left the stage. Ruby studied me then she and the others suggested I go talk to Shon. *Sure thing, I wouldn't have figured it out alone.*

The boy who had left to grab us drinks exactly half an hour ago, returned to us at that precise moment. I searched for something in my bag when my phone beeped. I had two unread message. The first one said:

"If you go to the cinema together, he'll talk so much that everyone around you will want to beat him up by the time the film is over. He has no idea what a beat is, he wouldn't even recognize it if he met it on the street. He's eco-conscious and a member of all the sects, you could call him a modern hippie."

The second message said this:

"Come to the entrance, now!"

I looked around, grabbed my bag and went outside.

Shon was waiting for me at the entrance outside. There was nobody in the street except for us. He didn't say anything, just walked towards me with deliberate steps.

"Amy, be honest with me! Are you ready to go out with me? Are you ready for me to propose to you someday in the future?"

"What's up with your girlfriend? The brown-haired goose?"

"Don't worry about her, I've dumped her. She was like a firework, only beautiful from a distance."

"I'm not even going to ask why you didn't call me. In any case, you didn't interest me enough to make me think about you for minutes, hours, or days!"

Shon let out a loud laugh and I tried to keep my serious expression until he leaned closer and kissed me.

"That's it? You kiss me and you think all is forgotten?"

"You weren't ready."

The complicated beginning reminded me of him. Of Adam. Maybe it was his kiss, maybe the fact that Adam and I had just recently said our goodbyes, maybe it was the air, or fate, but that strange night I'd fallen in love with him.

Three years flew by so quickly that I didn't even notice.

It was surprising even to me, but I was finally living in a happy relationship. Emphasis on the past tense because Shon was such a silly thing that he'd proposed to me and that's when everything started. Yes, everything, from the very beginning.

So, that's where we are now. In the present and I'm staring at my phone lying on the floor. I've stared at it so long that it finally started to ring. I watch it ring and ring until Holly shouts from the other room, telling me to answer it because she needs to sleep.

Let's have it over with.

"Yes?"

"Hi, Amy, it's Adam! I saw on the screen that you'd call us. I guess you wanted to talk to Ruby, but she isn't at home. Do you want me to give her a message? And please don't hate me so much that you hang up on me."

"I don't hate you. *Not anymore.* I've called Ruby because I wanted to tell her that I'm getting married. It's okay, I'll call her back later, or she can call whenever she gets back."

The line started to break up and it went quiet. I didn't want to call back, I didn't want to talk to Adam again. The phone rang a half an hour later. I answered more bravely than previously because I was convinced that it was Ruby calling me back. When I answered instead of Ruby I had Adam on the phone, again.

"Sorry, Amy, the call broke up accidentally."

I guess it broke up accidentally just like our relationship.

"Don't worry. I guess Ruby's still not at home?"

"No, she's not here."

We both sighed and I didn't really understand why he wasn't hanging up. After another long pause he spoke again:

"So you're getting married, huh?"

It was difficult to say yes. Even though I'd been with Shon for three years, Adam was still my first and in many ways the biggest love of my life. I love Shon and I'm in love with him, but Adam will always be Adam.

"Yeah, it seems so."

"It seems so? Someone has proposed to you, and you're walking down the aisle or you aren't?" he let out mocking laughter, then fell silent.

"Yes, I'm going to walk down the aisle."

"Huh. I don't know what one is supposed to say in this sort of situation. Congrats, I guess! When's the big day?"

"We don't have the exact date yet, but within the year."

"I have to go now. I wish you the best of luck."

He hung up even before I could've thanked him for his not at all honest good wishes.

I had to get it clear. I couldn't decide if Adam's behavior

was strange for me, or was he just really weird, in general? When I told Holly and my other girls what had happened, they didn't understand either.

Shon left for a week, he went on tour with his band, while I stayed home to work on an important project. My girls wanted to go out on the weekend, but I didn't feel like it even though there's no better time to let your hair down than when your boyfriend's just proposed, right? I decided that our wedding organization would be a perfect excuse not to go out, so I told my friends, who didn't know how to respond to my decision. It was true that we didn't have the exact date, but I still needed to search websites about wedding organization.

Looking at the bouquets, a lot of things came to my mind. Most of these 'lots of things' involved Adam and the past. *Our* past to be more exact. Just a few years ago, I was convinced that I'd only commit this sin, I mean getting married, with Adam. But here we were, in the present and I was about to say "I do" to Shon, and promise to stay with him until the end of our lives.

I was so lost in thought that I finally decided I needed some air. I wanted be alone and free like I was before all the years I'd spent with Shon, free from everything that reminded me of my life here. I grabbed a light summer jacket and headed out.

There was a fountain in our city and it was a favourite with tourists. No doubt, it was magical, so I went to see it at least once a week. There was a legend that the fountain would fulfil one of your wishes every year. I wasn't completely convinced about its effectiveness because my first wish was for Adam and I wanted to have answers about the two of us, but that's not what happened. And yet, I still made a wish every year. I hadn't used my wish this year and I wasn't sure what to ask for. I had a wonderful family, I had great friends, a promising future and a nice job. Not to mention the fact that I have someone who is really in love with me and he's a *real* person.

For heaven's sake, he's just proposed to me!

Yet, something stirred inside me. Something I only dared admit to the fountain. Usually, I stood in front of the fountain and talked to it as if it was a living, breathing, listening person. My first year with that poor fountain, it had to listen to all of my suffering about Adam. The second year, I also talked about Shon and naturally with the passing of each season, Adam's name came up less and less.

I liked to come here and watch the happy couples (of course I was unable to watch any of them until I got together with Shon, before that I used to hate them). I loved my time spent at the fountain and I'm not exaggerating when I tell you that I got the idea for most of my articles here. Honestly, I'm convinced that everything stable in my life is thanks to this fountain and its magic.

I wanted to make a wish, but I didn't dare. When we make a wish, we have to be honest to ourselves. Unfortunately, in the past few years I've often felt like I was living a lie. It's not like I wasn't madly in love with Shon, but Adam still lived inside me as if he was never going to leave.

I was searched for some change in my pocket because I wanted to make a wish. My life was about to change. I was about to enter a very new and serious period, but I felt like I couldn't do it. I managed to fish out five cent from the bottom of my pocket and I held it in my hand. I clutched it like I also had magical powers, but I knew I didn't. There was only one thing in my hand: a coin. I threw it in the fountain and made a wish.

After twenty minutes I headed back home. I felt better even though nothing had happened. I was standing beside the road when I saw... Him. He stood there on the other side of the road, leaning against a column, looking at the sky. I had to look twice to make sure it was really him. It was. He examined the sky, unmoving, and I watched him. Normally, my first question would be, what are you doing here, but now I could only think of one thing: My wish had come true!

He stood on the other side of the street, and years seemed

to melt away. I'm a bit ashamed to admit it, but there and then I forgot about everything else. Yes, even Shon. Adam stood there and I didn't care about anything else. *What the hell was happening?*

As I crossed over to the other side of the street, he walked towards me and hugged me without a question or a hello.

What could I have done? I did the thing my heart told me to: I hugged him back.

"Fancy a walk with me?" he asked as naturally as if it hadn't been three years ago since we last met.

"Sure."

The walk turned into a long talk which stretched well into the night. We talked about everything except us. He told me how he'd broken up with the brown-haired girl. I was so happy about it! I mean poor girl and stuff like that, of course, but still. I told him about Shon and I.

People used to tell me that if something's broke once, it could never be the same. Well, I beg to disagree.

Even after five year, my legs still trembled the same way when he was around me. My palms still got sweaty and my heart still beat so fast, I could barely breathe.

Yes, I was in love with Shon, but it was a completely different kind of love from the one I felt for Adam. I can't really explain or elaborate on this well. Even if I wanted to find a logical reason for my actions, I can't because it's just unexplainable even after all this time, I still wanted him.

After we talked through most of the night, I told him to sleep at our place. I didn't ask him why he came to see me because as an adult I saw through it. He obviously wanted to see me because somewhere deep down inside of him, he wasn't over me either. We went up to our flat, the others were back from the party, but luckily they were fast asleep. We sat down on the edge of my bed, quietly.

He took my hand, but didn't say anything.

I knew it wasn't right, but I had to kiss him, he had to kiss me one last time. Only one last time, he owed me this much.

"Adam, can I ask you to do something?"

I didn't even have to say it, he took my face between his hands and leaned closer:

"Are you sure you want this?"

"Yes," I said confidently.

Sadly, I admitted to myself that I answered this damned question with more confidence than when Shon asked me if I would marry him.

Adam kissed me, but after a few minutes I pushed him away. It wasn't right, I couldn't do this! It was the same kiss, the same feelings. He confused me. He didn't say anything, he just put his arms around me lamely. It was a lame situation, I was lame, everything was lame. Except for the kiss! I hated myself, nothing else happened.

In the morning when I opened my eyes, he wasn't next to me anymore. However horrible the situation was, I didn't start overthinking it. I didn't feel the same pain when he left for the first time. The first thing I felt was that it wasn't over yet. I sat up and I saw him sitting on the chair opposite the bed.

"I didn't want to wake you."

"Have you been awake for long?"

I asked the compulsory questions although I only cared about one thing: what the hell was really happening and why and the hell did this situation have to be so awkward?

"No, thank you. I couldn't sleep at all. I felt horrible and I felt like I didn't have the right to do *this*."

"*This*, what? If you mean the kiss, I'd like to remind you of one crucial detail: it was me who asked you to do it."

"I know, but it wasn't right. You know that too. I'll leave and you can continue living your life without me, as you've done before."

It's easy for you. You just go in and out of my life and you think it's okay.

"Why didn't you just leave? Why didn't you leave without a word like you did the last time?"

"Because I wanted to say goodbye."

"Adam, it's enough. You can't just leave again. We can't keep doing this until the end of our lives. Tell me that you don't feel this *thing* between us, and I'll accept it and let you go."

"Amy, you're getting married! You're going to be happy and I can't stand in the way of that. Shon is the right choice for you and not me. I don't know what got into me, I don't know why I came to see you. Maybe it bothered me that you belong to someone else, I don't know. One thing I do know however is that you should be with him and not with me."

His words had never broken me as much as they did now.

"If you really mean that, then just walk out the door. Walk away and never *ever* come back! Don't kiss me, don't feel anything for me! I know you're lying because you wouldn't be here, if it wasn't true!"

He ruffled his hair nervously then he stood up. He looked at me with tearful eyes and stepped towards the door. Before he closed it he looked back at me, but said nothing. Then he left, swiftly.

I can't cry, I can't cry, I can't cry.

Maybe he was right, I really am meant to be with Shon. Who knows and who decides? Apparently, he has finally decided for me.

After Adam left, I sat on the bed for a while until the girls came in my room to tell me about their night. I didn't tell them about Adam's visit and the fact that he crossed half the country to kick into me again. This too shall pass. Maybe he was right when he said a few years ago that I wasn't in love *with him*, but actually in love with our memories.

Although I don't quite know what he meant? The time when I woke up and found him gone after we'd finally gotten together or the moment when I saw him flirting with Cassie? I can't even be sure I know which beautiful memories inspire the most love for him in my heart.

Shon and I planned our wedding for the following summer. The next half a year, I spent all my free time organizing the wedding. My friends were a great help and Ruby also visited me quite often. I'd have never thought the biggest day of your life can be such a hustle. The flowers, the decoration, the dinner, the reception, the hen party and the stag. I really wanted everything to be perfect.

I imagined it with fresh flowers and a flower gate. Luckily, I'd made a few photographer and make-up artist alliances at the magazine, so I didn't need to waste any time finding those. Choosing the location created a certain number of problems: Shon wanted to have the wedding here, but my parents wanted me to get married in my hometown. What did I want? Just to get it over with. I pondered many times if I'd made the right decision. I was only sure about one thing, though. I didn't want to get married at home because that place reminded me of Adam and it always would. In the end I managed to convince my parents that the park with the fountain would be the perfect choice. Lots of celebrities had celebrated their weddings there and although I wasn't a celebrity, I felt like it would be the ideal place for us.

I let Shon choose the band who prepared a big surprise for our big day.

Before the wedding Shon had to go away, so I went to rehearsal with my friends. The venue was half ready when we arrived. I saw everything in my mind's eye: the flowers, the people dressed up in their best clothes and Shon. My only problem was that it wasn't going to be Adam standing there at the altar. After all these years it wasn't going to be him I'd say those three important words to, even though when I was a kid, I'd promised myself it would only be him.

I could imagine everything, except for me walking down the aisle.

Maybe that's only the panic talking.

I'd just sat down on one of the chairs, when Ruby told me we should start the rehearsal. I had nothing else to do, but walk down the aisle just as I'd do a week later. Holly was on the phone making arrangements for the flowers, when Cassie and Ruby gave me the sign. I was walking down the aisle when Holly got to her place. Cassie arranged the others and hurried forward.

Wedding rehearsal was on. I was walking towards the altar.

That's the exact route I'm going to follow. I'll have to concentrate not to step on the dress because if I do, I'll fall over. That can't happen. Don't worry, you'll manage.

That's where I'm going to say "I do." Then I'll step a bit forward and kiss him.

I looked over the rows. That's where my parents will stand and next to them, Shon's parents. Then Shon's friends and...

Time, through which I was happily marched towards the altar, seemed to collapse around me as if I'd been watching the movie of my life condensed into one minute. Every second was about the same person. Him. More precisely about my feelings for him.

In cases like this you usually hide your feelings. You hide them because you prefer to deny them, but then something unexpected happens. Years later, you see him again and you find it impossible that you feel the exact same thing for him, after all this time. But you feel it, very much. I stood there, ready to say goodbye to him and our six years, but I simply couldn't. I was unable to move forward. Because actually why should I? Oh yes, because I can feel him among the rows and I don't understand why. I don't understand what the hell's happening, how the hell is he able to watch me promise my life to someone else. I don't understand how it's possible for me to still see you as the same person after all this time? Why don't you change, why don't you get uglier, why don't you get out of my head already?

But you know what I understand the least of all? How we're still able to look at each other after all this time and feel even more indifference? It's as if years didn't pass us by, as if you and I were an item only yesterday. I carried all the anger and love of six years until this exact moment. Do you want to know what I think of this whole thing of ours? That this would be that specific situation when you have to say something, when you shouldn't let this thing happen, when you should create our happy ending, but you...

You, will always be you.

# Epilogue

## Book Launch

**Our guest: Adam Baker**
**The most famous bestselling writer of our time**

The audience grunted in unison.

"So, what happened to her in the end? Did the other guy marry her?"

A woman from the right side of the room violently interrupted the man reading.

"Are you kidding, you were madly in love, you didn't let her go, did you? You two were meant to be together."

"I agree with you. She left you too once, so now you have to call it quits," said a man in the crowd.

"I'm only interested in one thing: when you met her in that bar after all those years, you still loved her the same way you did when you were teenagers, didn't you?" asked a teenage girl.

"Do you still keep in touch?" came the barely audible question from the back row.

"Are you still shaken when people ask you about her?"

"Adam, why are you looking at the door so intensely?"

"Would you answer at least one of our questions?"

"Hey, are you still here? What's happening, why did you freeze like that?"

A female voice came from the entrance, most of the audience turned their heads in her direction because Adam's eyes had been on her for a while.

179

"Do you still love this girl?" asked the mysterious stranger leaning against the entrance.

The audience was agitated. Half of the people stared at the woman in the door, the other half waited for Adam's reactions.

"Do I love the girl who I stupidly followed to the altar? Maybe yes, maybe no. What do you think? Ladies and gentlemen, let me introduce you to the protagonist of all my novels, the girl who didn't try to change me, who accepted me for who I am, the woman to whom I finally managed to say those difficult three words to: I love you, Amy Baker.

# Acknowledgements

First of all, I'd like to thank my family who encouraged me from the very beginning. I'd like to say a special thank you to my brother for the wonderful cover. I'm grateful for my friends who have supported me from the get-go and assured me that they would surely buy my book even if they weren't going to read it. Of course, they were just joking. At least I hope so.

I'd like to also say thank you to my editor, "The Ballet Princess", for correcting my spelling, dedicating her time and energy to the project and also pointing out that actually some of the words I used didn't even exist. I'd like to thank my translator; without her work my dream would have never come true.

I left the most important for last: I'd like to thank my readers. I wouldn't be here without you. You were so eager to read the continuation of the story even when I only had one chapter. You were the ones who helped a simple blog story to become a book.

# About the author

I was never a good student in school and I always looked up to my classmates who had known from the very beginning what they wanted to be when they grew up. There were some who wanted to be teachers or flight attendants, while others planed to become a lawyer or a housewife. And me? I was hiding in the back row, worrying why I hadn't had any ideas yet. Then when I was around twenty, words started to pour from me and I knew that I had to write them down. I sent my stories to my best friends the next day. Their first question was: what book was it from? My lines seemed strange to me as well, it was hard to believe I'd written them. From that moment on I was writing night and day. I've had a lot of lame stories, misguided attempts, heart breaks and funny stories. At one point I realised that I have no doubts anymore: This is what I like doing. This is what makes me happy. I published my first book in the winter of 2014. Something has started, but it wasn't moving along. The feeling that there must be something more to life haunted me. My biggest dream was to see my first book in English. The tiny problem was that I had no money whatsoever. I packed my things and moved to England to save enough money. After three years and countless thoughts of abandoning I decided not to give up because if I didn't fight for my dreams, I could wave them goodbye. Nobody else was going to grab my hand and drag me after them.

Instagram.com/rileybakerauthor
Facebook.com/rileybaker

41562626R00103

Printed in Poland
by Amazon Fulfillment
Poland Sp. z o.o., Wrocław